As It Was . . .

As It Was . . .

Bruce Beaver

University of Queensland Press

Published by University of Queensland Press, St. Lucia, Queensland, 1979

Typeset by Academy Press Pty. Ltd., Brisbane
Printed and bound by Silex Enterprise & Co., Hong Kong
Designed by Cyrelle

Distributed in the United Kingdom, Europe, the Middle East, Africa, and the Caribbean by Prentice-Hall International, International Book Distributors Ltd., 66 Wood Lane End, Hemel Hempstead, Herts., England

Acknowledgments: Some of these poems appeared in earlier versions in the *Age*, *Nation Review*, *Southerly*, and the *Sydney Morning Herald.*

Published with the assistance of the Literature Board of the Australia Council.

National Library of Australia
Cataloguing-in-Publication data

Beaver, Bruce.
As it was.

ISBN 0 7022 1279 2 Paperback
ISBN 0 7022 1278 4

I. Title.

A821'.3

Contents

Also by Bruce Beaver:

Poems

Under the Bridge
Seawall and Shoreline
Open at Random
Letters to Live Poets
Lauds and Plaints
Odes and Days

Novel

You Can't Come Back

Thanks are due to Roger McDonald
whose interest in the tales of my childhood and youth
gave me the impetus to set it all down.

Thanks also to Tom Shapcott
whose inspired critical assistance
made the final shaping of this book possible.

Beginnings

for
Philip Benham

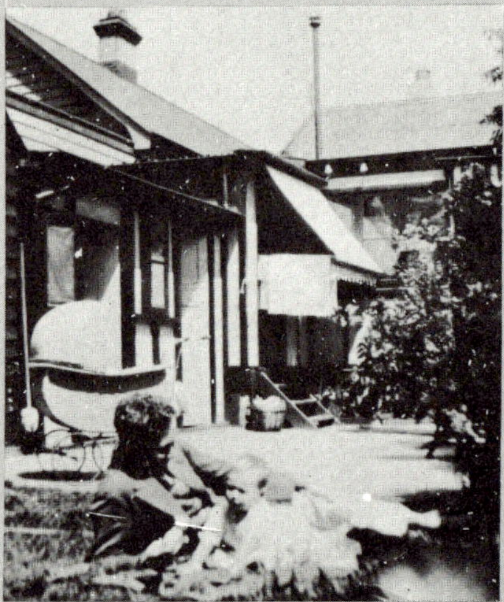

The First Paradoxical Memory

Your earliest memory may be of something
pleasant, an exotic taste or a pleasing
love releasing touch, or a sight
and smell of floral luxuriance. All
these in my own way I have shared
with you and the rest of the human world,
yet it remains to be said that my own
earliest memory was of something dead
although terribly alive at the same time—an
internal rhyme ticking alertly away
in a moribund verse. I won't come to the point
yet. You must imagine a big
(that is moderately sized) room in a huge
(that is medium sized) cottage hundreds of years
ago (that is more than forty and less
than fifty). I am very old at the time
(that is about three) and have reverted, because of
the crisply crushing beneath the knees
and splayed palms feel of the carpet, to crawling,
and have come vaguely and with purpose, aimlessly
and with infinite intent to the towering
cloud and timber capped doorway into
the always exciting, plushily inviting
lounge where my grandmother plays mah jong
with several almost untellable apart
lady friends with foxy furs
that snap jaws shut on foxy tails
and glare back in unwinking amber
at one if one strokes or rudely tugs.
The plump yet somehow petite group
of not completely grey grandmothers
in plainly cut yet finely shaped,
incredibly richly coloured dresses
of one colour, purple, midnight blue

or emerald, silk or moiré taffeta
would sit squatly yet strangely square
and upright, the spreading backsides balancing
more than amply developed busts.
And after the magical counters of bone
and bamboo with green and red inscriptions
were placed and the walls began to build
all would smoke the most amazing
cigarettes, gold tipped with the prettiest
cylinders of mauve and lilac,
crimson and yellow coloured paper.
I was allowed to watch from the always
open doorway—I can't recall
a closed door ever in that house.
I was allowed to watch QUIETLY,
that is I could make certain muted
noises and they may on occasion
reciprocate or somehow charmingly
ignore, according to what kind of
score they held. And sometimes I would
be offered a crème de menthe chocolate
or excitingly a sip from a bone white
demitasse of coffee which usually
made me cough and depart to the kitchen
for lemonade relief. And these were
my grandmother's modest matinées
and all her friends were surely my friends:
the tiny yet neatly rounded and chuckle-voiced
Mrs Alexander, the kindly Mo-nosed
and trumpeting Midge Levy (my grandmother
was née Rosamund Myer), the elegant
equine-featured always vivacious
Mrs Miles, and equally attractive
others. It seemed that none of them ever
fought or fell out among themselves
but one ought to entertain an at least
subterranean possibility of
such an inherantly human schism

occurring. I never witnessed what
I would have understood to be
an argument but sat amazed
in the doorway bordering bed and lounge rooms
watching the group at the green baize topped
collapsible card table play and smoke,
drink coffee and occasionally gin with something
added that I was allowed now and then
to sip, a letdown after lemonade.
To hear their fantastically blending converse
was my first inkling of the combining
tones of viola, violin, cello
and occasional brass. Was it always allegro
vivace or allegretto? It seemed so.
On other days—it must have been weekends
and Sundays for always on Saturdays
the phone attached to the dining room wall
was closely attended by him and the local
S.P. bookie—on Sundays then
the lounge was occupied by my grandfather
dressed in summer in cream coloured trousers,
cream shoes, cream silk shirt, with paisley tie
and socks to match, or in the winter
a flannel navy blue blazer and grey
trousers with black and brightly polished
shoes, the socks held up by suspenders
that only I and grandmother saw
besides himself. His friend McGain
and he would sit reclining or
in McGain's case hunched forward, talking.
Apparently McGain was in love with my grandmother
in an unreciprocal sort of way
but was amicably tolerated by both
grandparents. He was a large New Zealander
who manufactured and modified slightly
clothes mangles, refrigerators
and other unattractive machines.
I found him always off-putting and awkwardly

domineering, he looked like a brown
bear with thick glasses. He grunted at me.
He even grunted at my grandmother
and my mother and visiting father (my parents
were often "separated"). He boomed
interminably at my grandfather's
occasional asperities. Mac
was supposed to be somewhat deaf so he got
away with conversational murder.
But he and grandfather would sit and talk
and smoke Corona cigars from a fragrant
wooden box and drink amber stuff
that may have been White Horse or Johnny Walker.
And I would sometimes watch and listen
to their unintelligible talk,
but not as often as I watched
my grandmother's friendly mah jong games.
Grandfather then was the Lord Mayor's secretary
but in the Mayor's private enterprise,
the purveyance of canvas tents and blinds,
a large enough business to pay grandfather
twenty pounds a week which was then
more than enough to live on. It was
during the big depression and my
father and mother were poor and honest
but always well-fed as long as her parents
were in the offing. My father and grandfather
didn't "get on" but I was always staying
with my grandparents while my father tried out
a new job and mother roomed with him
until a new house was rented by them.
So the attractive house of my grandparents
was my home from home. On their cabinet
gramophone that had to be wound
I played and learned by heart such popular
masterworks of the Twenties as "It's
Hard to Tell the Depth of the Well
by the Length of the Handle on the Pump", and "Does

the Spearmint Lose its Flavour on
the Bedpost Overnight"; operetta
and grand opera. Galli Curci,
Richard Crooks, Caruso and Gigli,
the D'Oyley Carte Company and Soloists,
Tauber (or was it Crooks again?) singing
"You Will Remember Vienna" by Romberg,
and "Golden Days" from *The Student Prince*.
Later I graduated to yodelling
and cowboy songs, but then "Tit Willow"
could make me sad in a pleasant way
and "La Capinera" inspired me to learn
by heart and to whistle the flute obligato.
You say these are all happy memories
and so they are. They all have to do with
sitting or standing in the doorway
and only venturing into the lounge
when my grandmother played mah jong with her friends
or a grown-up was playing the gramophone.
The earliest memory is quite another
thing, the blackest of black comedies.
I'll tell you of it soon enough.
An episode brief and unforgettable,
endured alone, quite worthy of
a scene in a Henry James novella.
The facts are as follows: once upon a
moderately golden day when the generous
sun shone invitingly through the verandah's
mottled windows I crawled into
the unoccupied lounge and confidently
across the modified Persian-styled carpet,
between the looming blue and gold suite
of chairs and sofa, towards the far left hand
corner's small table upon which was placed
a shallow oblong lidded china
box within which were displayed in layers
my grandmother's highly glamorous
and multi-coloured cigarettes.

I had no intention of smoking one
but merely wanted to look at them closely
and maybe play with them as I played with
the pouch full of cribbage shells, the bridge
counters, the beautiful mah jong units
and numbered sticks of bone. Even the
domino sets made passable building blocks,
and all were in the lounge room in drawers
and cupboards or on the tops of tables
like the one I carelessly approached.
Then fire and acid pierced and burnt
through my right palm. I shrieked and sat up,
holding the hand before my eyes—
nestling furrily in its centre
was a dead bee whose living sting
had impaled by now my entire sensible
being. I wailed and stood and waddled
back through the bed and dining rooms,
down the stone steps, past the guardian trees,
the mandarin, the fig, the lemon,
to the back of the backyard where the clothes
were hung on the lines in front of the storage sheds.
I yelled and held up my invaded hand
to my grandmother who chid me for squashing a bee,
then saw that the bee was attached and brushed it
away still leaving the pain centering
my palm and consciousness. The fierce
assault on almost every receptive
nerve-end made me dance and howl
while grandmother hurried off in search of
tweezers and iodine. Hell was in all
the blue heavens and flapping soap-scented clothes
and thronged the very garden's flowers.
The house was no longer safe, the world
itself a place of torment. Soon
enough the sting was extracted and
the stinky liquid applied, but I
could not forget the spreading horror

of that pain, worse than the blue-bottled
nausea of castor oil or the whip
of live bluebottles at the beach.
I sat and sulked about it for
a day of ebbing agony.
In later years the only thing
that equalled it in torment was the
unanaesthetised reception of the
old foot-trundled drill of the dentist,
hot and sickeningly unbearable
with an aching, echoing aftermath
as dull and heavy as a tombstone.
So the first consecutively received
memories are of pleasure leading to
pain and utter helplessness.
In later years I thought of Maeterlinck's
male bee disembowelled in nuptial
flight, the queen bee trailing his streamers
of glory, the remnants of his intestines.
And though I respect the tiny, busy
fur-coated virginal executives
of the hive, I don't like them at all
or their process of continuity.
But I recall it was my queen bee grandmother
who eased the shocking sting and later
gave me a crème de menthe chocolate, so nothing
is irremediable, it seems.

Not being able to exact revenge is painfully frustrating to Christian
and non-Christian alike. To small children it is intolerable
and ultimately in a serious sense unforgettable.
But when a small child is placed in the horribly ambiguous position
of pointlessly hating a loved one or suddenly, bemusedly having to love
a hated one,
and what is worse losing all contact with the white and black of loving
and hating
and becoming suddenly, shockingly and inescapably conscious of
the normal and extending-into-infinity grey of the hating, loving
all-too-human condition, then sometimes the shock will alienate him or her
from himself, herself and indeed the whole human condition (albeit inwardly
and sufficiently hidden to bluff elders and youngers and even the medical
shamans
of the tribe for years, for a lifetime, for the forever of their remembered
existence
which is long enough for a small yet extended posterity).
Sometimes while visiting I
slept in the same bed as my grandparents. I realise now this may have
displeased
my grandfather which may have disconcerted my growingly voluminous
grandmother
both of whom were after all then only what used to be termed a middle-
aged couple.
Perhaps it was a midweek night and my grandfather agreeable to an
uninterrupted rest.
Whatever the prevailing mood of the double-bed's legitimate occupants
I was allowed
in, entertained to the glorious security of sleeping with loved ones, or at
the least,
familiar living bodies that the single child is inevitably deprived of. Even
the mousily or doggily scented presence of a younger or an elder brother
would have been appreciated, bad days and nights notwithstanding, as
for the almost

fragrant myth of a younger or preferably contemporaneous sister to sleep
with
or nearby, what winter hugging and summer touching seemed then possible
and
permissible. Of course I knew that elder sisters slept with no one else
but the occasional visiting girlfriend. Yet older girls had climbed under
the flimsy cover
of a verandah settee or couch on at least several occasions and had tickled
and played in a half-boring, half-arousing manner with me. So to be allowed
to share a bed for a night with my grandparents was very satisfying and
the end of a possibly perfect day. I had eaten on that particular evening
a good meal and fascinatedly watched grandfather rolling dry bread into
a heap of crumbs on his plate then mixing the lot into a malleable and also
edible blend. Then I had been allowed to listen to serials on the radio,
Chandu the Magician and perhaps *Frank and Archie* or *Following Father's*
Footsteps,
while I lovingly, almost gloatingly rubbed the small ounce block of fragrant
flake-cut
and darkly compressed pipe tobacco into a soft heap on a widespread
double page of the evening paper opened at the comic strips
in which Popeye shadowed by Poopdeck Pappy was having trouble with
the Sea Hag
again while Alice the Goon waited to be found on Goon Island, the Jeep
pointing the direction with Wimpy and Olive arguing as usual. I rubbed
gently
and devotedly the tobacco flakes, then—it must have been almost nine,
I sat awake and asleep on the floor in front of the big radio, a sort of
laminated temple with a veil never to be rent of fine brown cloth
across the speaker. The turning and the station selection were still almost
above my head but were no problem to my grandparents. I don't remember
ever being led to bed, guided or lifted, I only recall the briefest
touch of cool linen and of being folded into a time-machine of dreams
that floated and zoomed through the darkened cosmos of the oak-furnished
bedroom. Well I knew
the separate pieces of furniture: to the right of the double bed which faced
the cream coloured wooden wall was a lowboy in which was kept my
grandfather's clothes
and shoes and ties and in a top compartment a bottle of White Horse whisky

or Johnny Walker, one at a time, he alternated apparently.
I liked the White Horse best because of its little thimble cap that could
be used as a cup, and was, though never by me. I couldn't reach that high.
And behind the bed's head between two windows and against the farther wall with a walking
space between it and the bed was the big dressing table with drawers too heavy
to pull out and a wonderful array of cut glass jars and stoppered bottles
and a tray on which the beautiful silver-backed brush and comb set lay, beneath
two small side drawers full of cosmetics, powders, rouges and lace handkerchiefs
and above these drawers the room-reflecting mirror that stiffly swung to whatever
required angle. Then to the left of the bed against the windowed wall
a lounge chair and a medium-sized wardrobe of dark brown veneer
and massively against the other wall the most tremendous wardrobe ever
built to meticulous order, it could be disassembled and reassembled
with ease. Finally to reconstruct that once-upon-a-time room in a
house no longer standing, in the far right corner across and away
from the bed's head was another chair and beside it and under a framed print
of King Cophetua and the Beggar Maid my grandmother's cloth, linen, memento
crammed and naptha mothball scented ottoman. Even in the dark
I knew where everything was. Elsewhere we seemed never to stay long enough
to get to know the place or people. My father was a travelling salesman
and already the depression had made this job more competitive than he was inherently
or ever wanted to be. A gentle man inclined to fits of melancholy
which erupted into alcoholic denunciations of the country's
nominal leaders, and manic musings on those substantial shadows that
the scurrilous *Truth* threw across his bed each Sunday morning: The Pyjama Girl,
Woolcott Forbes et al. My father had lost his youth in the First World War
spending his seventeenth and eighteenth years in France, in mud, under bombardment.

His schooling had been that of trench warfare and the knack of quick
inebriation.
He came back to one fat cheque and a year of party and theatre going
with mother;
probably the happiest time of both their angst-ridden lives. After this they
were
engaged for another eight years. In their own way both were gluttons
for pleasure and punishment.
The remnants of their generation, like mine, led totally bewildered lives.
So surrounded by a probably spurious undoubtedly short-lived sense of
security
I nestled and roamed dreaming in my grandparents' double bed on her side,
on the outside edge. Nothing and nobody ever would come between them.
The dark
inside the room was full of habitual comforts of feeling and resting
refreshingly.
In the outer dark flitted and fretted Count Dracula, and awkwardly yet
unavoidably roamed
Baron Frankenstein's monster, Fu Manchu and the more than living
inventions of Poe
and Wells, unread as yet but radio-amplified and starkly filmed.
It must have been towards dawn for when I unhappily woke the room
was lightened.
In my dream I had been constantly tormented by a contemporary, small
enough
to fight back at, large enough to hurt, yet passively accepting. The goading
and finally the blows got to me, stinging, humiliating. I could not get away
from my tormentor. He intended to go on hurting me until I was
obliterated.
It was now a matter of life or living death. In screaming rage and hatred
I threw myself towards him, pummelling and kicking. I knew no fear
only the insatiable
desire for revenge. I would destroy his hold over me and considerably
damage him
in the process. As he backed a little, giving ground I pursued him
frenziedly,
unstoppably as Hake the Berserker in R.M. Ballantyne's *Erling the Bold*.
Hake who fought on furiously, wielding his gigantic double-bladed sword

after both his legs had been cut off. In truncated but fanatical rage
overflowing with the adrenalin of righteous indignation I forced
my tormentor into a corner and fell on him like something out of a saga. I beat
and beat and gouged and kicked, feeling the blows strike home with hurt and knew
the growing satisfaction at beginning to win over a loathed enemy.
And then I was shaken awake by a drowsy, chucklingly complaining grandmother
who didn't want her tummy kicked in or her bosom dented, as she put it.
I fell away from her in an admixture of the painfullest love and bitterest chagrin.
I wept into the pillow and onto the sheets. I literally wet the bed
for the first time in so many years I had forgotten when, and so awake,
both wide and deluge-eyed with the most intense frustration I had ever known
clashing with bitter shame and guilt and sorrowful love. Where had he gone,
my enemy? Into her shape? Was he mocking me as her? Grandfather snored on gently
while grandmother quickly drew my grizzling and shaking nightmare ridden self to her
capacious and undeniably real being. We both fell asleep again.
And though I was then untroubled by further bad dreams, on waking and ever afterwards
things were never to be the same again. It was all odi et amo
overlapping, frustrating and alienating; waking or sleeping, a botched world.

My first day at school in the early Thirties was unforgettable mainly because it was the first and last for at least another year.

I was perfectly content to "loaf and invite my soul" in my sixth year in the not to me straitened circumstances of my parents' cottage rented from my grandparents, halfway down the northern slope of Red Hill overlooking Manly and about three quarters of a mile from Fairlight Private Hospital where I had been born. The cottage near the beginning of one of the longest streets in Manly fronted towards the hilltop Fire Station and the shopping centre: a panoramic view of the wholly inimitable harbour and the sentinel heads, one high and craggy, one low and rising gradually to a lighthouse. These opened onto the everlasting, everywhere reaching Pacific. The cottage backyard and the back window faced north to the elegantly established golf course that on wet days and in generally stormy weather was white with myriads of seagulls facing all the same way into the wind and rain. To the right, on another hill that blocked Ocean Beach from sight, a sandstone house; behind it three tall pines.

The cottage from road level fell twenty feet so that the backyard was reached by a steep flight of wooden steps, and under the house was an open basement and the lavatory. In this area and beneath the house and about the stone foundations my neighbourhood friends and I played out our tenuous encounters.

Later we lived a little further along the street in a wooden house ominously named "Stone End" but that was in Thirty-Seven, year of the first Buck Rogers books, and also the year in which I witnessed an epileptic girl in a fit of petit mal on returning from church, twitching and gasping on the side of

the road while an adult watcher remarked "She's wound up" and I thought "She's wound down," but both of us were wrong.

In the year of my first reluctant day at school, Balgowlah Public, not far on past the cemetery fringed by the pavement-shading pepper trees, but at five and something years another part of a big country out of range of calls to a parent and grandparent, and who else was there to call to? The numerous elder cousins were kindly enough but never very close, not even at the legendary weekend picnics at idyllic North Harbour where I began to dream awake on sunstruck, smouldering or sparkling days of jade and amethyst waters salt-savoured, of grey-pocked rocks draped over with seaweed amber and green, scabbed with oyster and winkle shells traversed by tiny crabs inhabiting pools of salty sand-based clarity, skirting the crimson sucking mouths of sea-anemones. And over the glittering blue-glazed bay the wharves, the pines, the shops and orange tiled housetops of the village Manly.

I had been up to this age content to sit through mornings shaping entities out of fragrant glitterwax that was not really malleable, and smelly old plasticine that was, or piling building blocks that clicked and clunked together agreeably, and in the everlasting afternoons had sprawled half-dazed with the innate propriety of siesta before the small and muffled sounding "wireless set", relishing the "mulberry tones" of the West Indian singer Turner Layton gently crooning the pop song "Home", or as I knew it then "When Shadows Fall", and sometimes hearing the top hit with the "kiddies", "The Toymaker's Dream"—I even knew the words: "A jolly little workman was making toys all day". I pictured something like Laurel and Hardy's version of Victor Herbert's *Babes in Toyland* in which the impossible Stan manufactured a batch of two hundred six foot toy soldiers instead of six hundred two foot dittoes and marvellously saved Toyland from the gorilla-like demons yet could not prevent big Ollie from getting an ultimate arsefull of cannon fired darts. But the days were long and my mother knew I should be among other growing children so dragged me protestingly up to the Balgowlah School Principal's office one callously sunny day, and as I sensed and smelt the chalk and ink-fouled reek of school, I knew what otherwise bewildered animals sense on the ramp within the slaughterhouse.

The Head was a Head Mistress and quite reasonably affable, that is while my mother remained. She picked me up squirming and finally in controlled desperation took me to see a gigantic phallocentric pea-pod made out of green glitterwax. Her apparent admiration of it unnerved me. I think I kicked her before she put me down. And when the very last hope of survival departed from me (I wonder was that when the overweening sense of betrayal began to fester, lasting over half a lifetime?), she abruptly had me taken from her transformed presence and placed among a classful of my gloating or detached contemporaries and one thin, bespectacled female adult who scared hell into and out of me by reciting "The Town Musicians of Bremen" so vividly that I panicked like the townsfolk in the tale and made a tearful break for it but was restrained gently but firmly, in the operative phrase. I lasted until the lunch-hour when my woollen winter underpants unrolled and hung down far beneath my shorts. Surrounded by children I was pointed at, laughed at, mocked, and finally pushed around a bit.

I cleared out while the supervising teacher was bleakly ordering my bullying classmates and others to put all egg shells, orange peels and apple cores into the nearest rubbish bin. I fled and did not pause in flight even to attempt to roll up the offending underwear. I sobbed in panic flight beneath the winter sun and fifteen minutes later was ensconced inside the basement lavatory at home, walled round by damp and sympathetic mossy rock, too constipated to relieve myself but grateful to be home again. I finally ventured up the wooden stairs and blabbed out my embarrassment, my shame and fierce resolve never to return to that or any other "public" school, which may have had some small effect on next year's firm decision to enrol me at St Mary

Immaculate's, the only local Catholic school, which was as horrible in its own way as any other school could be in those long, dreary days of canes and leather straps and government sanctioned baby-bashing.

All my memories of schools were discoloured by the omnipresent tint of
fear.
Of the several good and kindly teachers out of dozens of others best
forgotten, one relinquished the work,
one retired prematurely
for me if not for him,
and the kindest simply died of alcoholic complications.
My schoolfellows were a majority of monsters with a very small minority
of fellow-sufferers and eccentrics.
God help them; if they live, how do they live?
I never expect to see again anyone from those days
of almost continual nausea and apprehension.
I could read before I went to school.
I have duly learned everything else I needed to know
to more-than-survive in life and the arts
since leaving those crapulous institutions.

What is it on earth that keeps a child alive besides food and drink and much parental affection? Fantasy, of course, as it must and always will be—sheer, inventive fantasy, the child's own wild garden of ever budding imagination. Some, like Milton and Toynbee, lisp in numbers and languages and are fired into an even more fantastic youth and an imaginative adult life by the quite obsessional administrations of a truly zealous and highly literate guardian or parent. My early tutors were the abominable, the magnificent media of the comic book, the radio, the film. They fed me unendingly the fantasy that I was avid for. While popular music soothed or greatly excited my none-too-savage breast, they lit the way through greys and reds and blacks and whites of days.

At the age of seven I saw unattainably through a shop window the egregious Billy Bunter on a blue and orange cover of the *Magnet* hauled up from an ocean-pounded cliff's ledge by his always begrudging companions, the Famous Five, the would-be victims of his interminable congame. I gazed and spelled out the caption: "Will the Rope Break?" And underneath the question: "Weight and Sea"—my first memorable encounter with a literate pun. Though I hadn't money to buy the comic I felt that I'd made an unforgettable discovery. Later I alternated *Magnets* and *Gems* with their formulary circuses of clowns, monkeys, lions, elephants, gymnasts, aerialists, ringmasters, all disguised as impossible British schoolboys and their obnoxious teachers with varietal fare full of heroes and villains and too few girls (I sneakily read the *Anne* and *Emily* books for these) with other weeklies *The Triumph* and *The Champion* with heroes like the Black Hawk (El Halcon Negro) and Rockfist Rogan R.A.F. whose machine guns went rat-tat-tat-tat while deadly Jerry bombs went wheeeee-crump! And even more adventurous *The Hotspur's* Iron Teacher—was it a robot? Or was he a man in the disguise of a robot? And SF too, "The

Lost School on the Whirling Planet". Pretty dicey this one; the boys were kidnapped for breeding purposes by the sterile hominids. And before all these the non-stop vaudeville in pictures of the English *Comic Cuts*, *Funny Wonder*, *Chips* and the really streamlined *Film Fun* with its ingenious cartoons of Laurel and Hardy, George Formby and so many others.

But most exotic of all were The American Comics which began to appear in 1938 preceded by booklength printings of daily strips of Buck Rogers whose stunning rocket guns went Zap! and whose disintegrators went Br-r-rup! and Felix the Cat whose burrowing machine made it to the hollow centre of the earth populated by elves, then stopped in an underground cave glittering with huge and shapely diamonds (I never fully understood why the machine stopped there and simply didn't go on burrowing until it emerged on the other upside down side of the earth—I'm sure there were no controls). And Hurricane Hawk who flew all over the place chasing a villain who had one hooked non-hand and who when shot and buried in a shallow grave dug himself out many hours later (he wore a bulletproof vest) after cleverly practising "breath control". But next to the great Buck Rogers most popular of all was dot and dash-eyed Popeye and his fabulous companions: Olive, Wimpy, Rough-house, Swee-pea, Oscar, Toar, the Goons, the Jeep and Poopdeck Pappy, and the wholly black-garbed George W. Geezil who said in fury things like "I hate you to pieces!" and "You are the flies in my zupe!" while J. Wellington Wimpy intoned while slavering over a hamburger (that meal in epitome of a world-wide depression) "My friend, you are the salt of the earth, the gem of the ocean." Popeye's most notable enemies were Bluto, the Sea Hag and the horned Demings. But the brightly coloured American Comic Books ("64 pages for 6 pence") teemed with fantasy so varied and memorable: *Famous Funnies* had Buck Rogers in colour and The Captain and the Kids, while *Tip Top Comics* had Tarzan and the Katzenjammer Kids which were the same as the Captain and the Kids only different. And so many other scintillating titles with pages of Li'l Abner and Alley Oop the caveman, and utterly crazy beings like Smokey Stover the Firefighter whose boss Firechief Cash U. Nutt would explode apart in atomic reaction and whose set of dentures in mid-air would exclaim "Well, starch my cravat!" and whose station walls were always liberally hung with the framed and unforgettable word "Foo". And dear, vulnerable, yet always surviving Krazy Kat and her inimitable partners in love-hate games, Ignatz Mouse and Officer Pup and nasty Mrs Kwak Wak. I memorised a passage out of Krazy which she soliloquised one mauve evening in the Oy Vay Mesa. It was a poem beginning "I are illone jetz me an jetz my dee dee diary". Truly I lisped in balloons. I even remembered the local advent in Woolworths of all places of Superman who looked then like a school inspector wearing trapeze gear.

Besides all these there were the ritualistic Saturday afternoon movies (or flicks as we called them long before disembowelling was everywhere in fashion). To summon up a Saturday afternoon programme is not impossible: Episode Seventeen of *Flash* (called Speed in the Sydney papers because Flash meant a lair—now Speed means dope. So much for current slang) *Gordon* followed by several Paramount Popeye cartoons, a Hopalong Cassidy or Gene Autry western in which the hunted and the hunters raced on horses round one large and rugged rock unendingly while firing fusillades into the air before or after which The Sons of the Pioneers sang "Cool, Clear Water" or "Wagon Wheels" or "Tumbling Tumbleweed". Then after interval and the unintelligible microphone address from the stage by Uncle This or That announcing the envied holders of the prize-winning-lucky-numbered-ice-cream-bucket-top would come the piece de resistance with Laurel and Hardy, The Marx or Ritz Brothers, or Boris Karloff with about an hour of comedy or horror.

Lastly, the radio serials, even more intimate and largely I realise now, local products: Dad and Mum and Dave and their galloping theme "Gundagai" which could be played slowly when pathos predominated, for instance, a prize cow down with milk fever. The interminable *Search for the Missing Link* (Growl, growl, crack, screech, "Good Shot, Professor!" followed by its theme music, the beginning of Pierne's "Entrance of the Little Fauns"); *High Frequency*, a science fiction thriller ahead of its time in which a young Jack Davey always seemed to be having the screaming mimis; *Yes, What?* a kind of antipodean Will Hay school where Dr Percy Pym walloped Greenbottle whose cacophonic voice, half screech, half croak was and is unique, while vulgar Bottomley and softy Stanford made up the three types of schoolboy, asinine, criminal and the merely very dull; the years' long *Search for the Golden Boomerang*, "The Dance of the Sugar Plum Fairies" its pretty theme; *Martin's* (long suffering) *Corner*, a small atypical grocer's shop whose halfpenny-splitting crises were introduced by "The Music of the Spheres"; fantastically deployed "Till Eulenspiegel" ushered in Old Nancy, Witch of Salem, and Satan her caterwauling Tom o'Bedlam, in *The Witch's Tales*, forbidden yet irresistible.

All these kept fantasy alive and made living almost bearable and something like an adventure on a Christmas holiday throughout a year of bellyaches and homework designed to kill the fancy and strain weak eyes. Without these bright, unsubtle panaceas aesthetically on a par with an all-day-sucker revealing rainbow layered bitter dyes that tasted bad but looked magnificent, how many of us stranded in the Thirties in ennui and the agonies of childhood could have survived with whole imaginations?

My appendectomy was put off for a month because I had a slight cold in the head. At ten I wasn't popular among my nominal peers at school and everywhere else who at the best of times were barely tolerant because I wore glasses and read a lot without relating to them what I greedily read. So for several happy weeks I stayed close to home and played sporadically with curious acquaintances and my almost friend McDermott who was gentle faced, curly haired and stubborn as a bull calf. I kept on calling him Ron or Mac when all the others called him Ming, after Ming the Merciless in *Speed* (Flash) *Gordon*.

He would come and play with me on the beach. We would carefully build rocket ships out of sand and fire away at each other (he had a Buck Rogers rocket pistol, I had a disintegrator). There was some uneasiness here, my gun had cost a lot more than his and this seemed to embarrass him so that he stressed the better quality of his gun's performance. It went Zap! like they did in the comic strip and what's more it fired match sticks out of the barrel. Mine lit up faintly on top and made a rather ineffectual buzzing noise, a ping, certainly not a Br-r-rup! He called it a bruptegrator and probably liked the bizarre look of it. I'd have swapped guns anyday with him. Later I was given at Christmas a Liquid Helium pistol which impressively fired fifteen shots of water melting effectively the sand structures we built.

But in 1938 while waiting to go to a hospital miles away from home for the operation I was told not to play too roughly and one day was thoroughly scragged on the beach by several healthier enthusiasts and came limping home with a pain like a stitch in the right side which was altogether wrong so I was banned from beach forays. I tried to explain that Foxy, another almost intimate, had leapt bare-footed onto a broken bottle, spilling much blood, and had needed to be accompanied home where he was bandaged and boxed about the ears by his small and eternally harassed mother. It seemed to me he was that much more worse off than I was but the ban remained and in a week I was hospitalised.

There the appendectomy was postponed for another week as I still had a head cold that could cause surgical complications. I was in a huge ward that stretched for miles it seemed on either side of my unusually high bed. On my left was a very attractive elderly gentleman who kindly talked with me when I was very much alone and showing it. One evening he took a small tube from his locker and squeezing from it what he called Goosegrease proceeded to carefully wax and point his moustache with it. This enchanted and distracted me. To my right was another elderly man, though highly irascible and physically unattractive. He was not gentle yet displayed a grudging concern for my discomforts. When the nurse perched me on a bedpan in full view of the disinterested ward I was constipated with shame and this cranky old one-eyed man who seemed to be full of pain raised himself up and bellowed for a screen to be placed around my bed. He roared out "The poor kid's sitting up like Jacky on a rock". So I was curtained off and still couldn't do a thing until I was given an enema. Some days later there was a screen around the old pirate's bed and a transparent tube hanging down that dribbled dark urine into a bottle. Then somebody else I don't remember was in the old man's bed or maybe it just stayed empty.

Across the ward a young man lay "swathed in white linen". He had twenty-four new stitches in him and looked tired. Next to him was the afflicted joker of the ward, an ebullient lanky young clown of a man whose one professional aim was to make the stitched one laugh at his continuing jokes because it hurt the other when he laughed. Not that the joker was sadistic. It simply fascinated him to be beside the living embodiment of the subject in the joke that ends "It only hurts me when I laugh". So all afternoon he joked and cajoled and was scolded by nurses but achieved only the wannest of smiles from the bandaged young man. Then simply on the spur of the moment, merely for relief I'm sure, the joker farted so loudly and protractedly, so quaintly in that the wind breaking played a definite tune like an unskilled bugler practising scales, that from one end of the usually solemn ward to the other uproarious laughter and loud applause broke out while the joker fell across his bed as if shot. Then the bandaged young man began to laugh until he cried, then laughed again and in the process broke all twenty-four stitches and was wheeled away still giggling uncontrolledly while the remorseless joker was "severely reprimanded" by several smiling nurses and one unsmiling sister, and lay back in fulfilled triumph on his ever-rumpled bed.

Then it was time for my operation. The doctor was young, red-haired and friendly. I started counting to ten and then was being helped to frothily regurgitate hours later in my seemingly new bed by my smilingly anxious mother. I had a slight soreness in my right side and a large new Popeye comic with a loved creature in it, Eugene the Jeep which always told the truth by bowing down and pointing its tail upward, except when distracted by June bugs which caused it to bow down and point its tail upward and which had nothing to do with the truth.

For another week I lay in bed and watched the nurses come and go (most surprisingly in the dark of four a.m. when they hoisted you up out of sleep and rubbed your back raw with methylated spirits just to discourage bedsores). They eventually got around to unwinding my belly's bandage and snip snip the two (two only!) stitches from the inch long scar. The skilful doctor had apparently managed the smallest appendix incision on record locally so he would be congratulated and I was bound to be almost ignored (my tiny scar that is) by unenthusiastic school-fellows, all of whom would feel let down, even cheated. Foxy's footsole would have needed at least six stitches. On the way back home to Manly the maniac taxi driver frightened everyone by his overfast, erratic driving. I was obviously back and incomplete at beginnings again.

The First Death

Grandfather's first and second strokes came towards the ending of the last year of the Thirties, the last year of "peace" and the decade-long depression. I should have known better but when they told me that he had entered into a state of second childhood I honestly imagined he would get better and play with me like a brother, another child, instead of a rather distant and apparently coolly natured, notably elder, relative. It seems that several years prior to his collapse, I had displeased him over something—some rudeness to my mother, his daughter, I think it was—and he had put me almost out of mind and heart; so that when he fell down in the backyard garden trying vainly to attach a recalcitrant length of hose to a low placed tap, and thereafter had to be kept in bed all the time, and while in bed was stricken a second time so that he lapsed into a senile condition and lay all day uncovered on the double bed like a large and hairy baby, I felt sorry for him in a strangely distanced way. He kept on kicking off his pyjama trousers so that his old man's genitals were constantly in view and they were, to say the least, quite adequate. Or had been; their grey-haired flaccidity was carried through to the facial features, his shapely lips once so firmly set beneath his moustache slobbered and his eyes rolled like a new-born baby's.

His house nurse was a very attractive, youngish woman who seemed most of the time to be wearing a pink slip or a peignoir that accentuated the loose but slimly curved lines of her body. I knew she was married to a short and anxious older man in a soldier's uniform. His name was Os and she obviously didn't love him. He visited once. And once on another occasion she watched me through the door of the backyard shed while I was playing obsessional games and talking to my selves. I saw her pink gowned figure poised not at all pryingly outside the shed attentive to my talk and with a concerned expression on her gently attractive face. She asked me questions when I came outside and I told her of my creepy little games and doubtless helped her to a not-too-late interest in child psychology. My grandmother liked her until the night she interrupted the nurse and a business partner of my grandfather's passionately kissing in the lounge room. I think the nurse was discharged and the partner lapsed from a family friend to an acquaintance. Several months later I passed his place and saw him propped in an invalid's chair in the sun and wearing a dressing gown over a full pair of pyjamas but gazing vacantly before him, his mouth slackly opened. It was a bad year for strokes.

But it was towards Christmastide upon a Saturday afternoon that grandfather died. Evidently my grandmother had heard the rattling change of gears in his breathing that she had known was the sign death had begun the parking of the body. I was at the "flicks" with Mac and we had relished Laughton hamming it up with an obviously false aquiline beak as Sir Humphrey Pengallon in *Jamaica Inn*. We'd been impressed by Newton's rolling eyes and "r's" and Emlyn Williams' tight-arsed bloody-minded little smuggler. There was a girl in it too, beautiful dark-eyed Irish Maureen O'Hara making her debut. We would remember the screams of the shipwrecked men slaughtered by the smugglers and the big bang of the pistol going off in Newton's face, and Laughton descending with the camera at so many tens of feet per second—Mac knew—from the mainmast crow's nest: "Make way for Pengallon!"

So I'd come back to a house of hushed mourning and grandfather's body quiet and sheeted over. When I looked at him the only difference seemed his hands and legs were still and his mouth and eyes closed. I was told to go to the grocer's and buy a half pound of butter. When I was snapped at for something or other by one of the smart alec assistants I said "My grandfather's dead. I'm not in the mood for argument" and left them with that lethal flea in several ears. True, I must have been insufferable, but so were they. I was full of a very special kind of self-importance: I carried news of death like a white-paper wrapped slab of cold, hard butter straight from the freezer.

When I returned I realised I had not cried or wanted to cry, though I had liked and respected my now more than alienated grandfather. My mother boiled me an egg and I ate it with bread cut in strips and smeared with some of the butter, with pepper and salt mixed on the saucer's rim and a cup of milky tea. I think she ate an egg, too, but my grandmother ate nothing then and little later for several days, making do with tea and aspirin powders and an occasional cigarette. She didn't grieve loudly or very obviously at the time but I knew she'd been crying and would cry again and again over the coming days and nights. I hugged and kissed her but my thoughts were preoccupied with two possible Christmas presents, scale models of an anti-aircraft gun with units of gunners and a field gun that fired thin steel shells a distance of six feet away and accurately enough to knock a toy soldier down. By the following year my father would join up with an ack-ack company and then transfer to transport while I played with scale model heavy duty army lorries and detachable though rigidly squatting drivers. Within another year he'd be shipped to Malaya where after months of golf and drinking parties at the nineteenth hole followed by one too many servings of nasi goreng his long suffering incipient ulcer would erupt and he be invalided back to Australia and there demobbed (he was over forty) some months before Malaya fell to the Japs. But now he was still a toll collector on the Harbour Bridge and working through most nights, sleeping most days, which was better than selling something somewhere sometimes.

Sitting and dreaming about the Christmas presents I suddenly remembered my late grandfather taking a Buck Rogers book from me some months before to see if it was "suitable". It had an extended episode in which Wilma Deering lost her clothes while taking a dip on Saturn or somewhere and moved about or posed nakedly through several pages. He gave it back to me without a word. He was not that kind of hypocrite, having enjoyed it himself. I settled near to the turned down radio set and opened the evening paper soundlessly—the thought of rubbing no more pipe tobacco brought a pang—at the latest episode of Popeye's strange encounter with the Demings who lived beneath the ground and pulled "cababbages" out of the farmers' mouths into their own. It did not hold me as the earlier adventures. It seemed my memories were all of several years before when in that room so redolent of tasty food and pipe smoke I'd crouched where I sat now, fighting off sleep imprinting on my mind the scenes and sayings in Popeye's search for his reluctant Poppa.

Flying

We had a problem in our family now, actually it was my father's problem but as he was a living presence once again among us it became a family problem. Simply he drank too much at weekends and was inclined to be irascible sometimes during the week. He knew my mother and I neither loved nor respected him despite his attractive appearance or popularity at the Saturday pubs. This was before I had to bail him regularly out of goal each week on Sunday mornings with a ten shilling note a regular "part of the pattern", as practising sociologists, psychologists, advertising executives and other collectors of such phrases are inclined to say.

He was invalided from the army to live with us when I was still thirteen and attending Sydney High on something like false pretences (I was quite incapable of learning anything but French phrases and passages of music by heart). I would leave in a year in disgrace, in relief. But my benighted father who was an essentially kind man could not come home to the shared asperities of insecure wife and upstart critic child so was driven on to argue almost interminably with us both, singly or together —"a classical case" as the sociologists etcetera would probably say. Of what? Of obvious incompatibility—of an innate fear of life borne with bravely enough—of an Australasian male's incontrovertible right to seek companionship verging on all but oblivion with and among his own sex as sad and sexless boys in the reiterated ceremony of mateship; all the golden hours relived of golden youth and golden beer—the iron pyrites of hangover and worse: the slow corroding ulcer, the fat-congested heart, the starved, cirrhotic liver, the self-encouraged cancer. Among these stricken boys who had behaved like men in bed, on battlefield, before the sleek or gaunt employer, yet never once within their heart of hearts; who knew the world so well, yet no jot of themselves, my father moved and had his being, and was loved.

And so it seemed my mother had no husband and I no father "to relate to" as the sociologists etcetera and newspapers uphold glibly. Without a doubt I did not want to assume the role of manhood (hairs within my armpits and about my genitals). I unhesitantly shaved the latter's first growth clean, "simulating emasculation" according to all the sociologists etcetera who seemed to live most of my life for the next unlucky seven years. But the prickly then luxuriant growth soon reasserted itself and I forbore merely to strip in front of younger boys. Just as preoccupied with sex as any other satyr of a similar age no exhibitionist tendencies existed for me then or now. But music. And the reading of countless books and comics. These became obsessional. And falling long and faithfully in love with certain film stars seemed to be quite apart from sex, though all were "inter-related" as the etceteras would say.

Early on one particular mid-week evening I was sprawling on my kitchen bed which served also as a couch, placed beneath the big window. The procedure on all weekends was simple, my mother and I took flight on Saturday afternoons to my aunt's house a mile away at Balgowlah. We'd return the next morning but my father would spend the day in bed and not get up until Monday. Perhaps this night he'd skipped the evening meal. For some reason he'd begun to harangue my mother and me, but this time I refused to listen, burrowing my nose into a Buck Rogers comic in which something rather horrible had just occurred. Buck had investigated a melted rocket ship and looked down in horror and pity upon the luckless pilot whose slumped back was facing the inventive reader. I could imagine without much effort the pilot's face resembling a Christmas ham overlaid with glazed crackling, or maybe a distorted charcoal mask, the ship's instruments had dripped into stalagmites of steel and bubble shapes. I was really consciously ignoring my father's berating but was hypnotically drawn to the comic's happenings.

My father strode across the room to my bed and seizing the comic book from me, hurled it through the open window into the night outside. Without a thought I leaped after it through the window and onto the lavatory roof a foot or two below then jumped about another eight feet into the backyard, rolling on grass and clay and grabbing at my comic.

Almost immediately my father had launched himself out of the window and bounced off the roof to land beside me and inspect me for breaks or bruises, the while warning me never to do such a thing again while he, the rentpayer, was talking to me.

I wept and groaned a bit and he accompanied me up the wooden stairs and back into the kitchen where my mother made a pot of tea for us all, shaking bewilderedly her dark head at the peculiar misfortune that had landed her with a brace of aerobatic madmen.

Remembering those moments I think the mantel radio was playing a then quite popular version of the "Spinning Chorus" from the *Flying Dutchman*. I'd learnt that year a fourth part ("Round and round my wheel goes whirling . . .") but I'd envied the firsts who'd had the attractive melody. When we re-entered the room my mother had switched off the set. She wanted no background music for further melodramatics. I think the jump had shaken up my middle-aged father more than myself for he quietened down for the rest of the evening but I tucked Buck Rogers beneath the cover of the couch and drank my tea and listened attentively to my parents drinking theirs in silence.

When they went to bed I lay under the window in star-winking and moon-lightened darkness. My heart raced on at the thought of my unthinking leap into "outer space" without a flying-belt, and of how gently the grass and cushioning clay received me, and also of how not one of our neighbours had noticed the flying father and son from their seasonably opened yellow and amber lit windows. And how I had felt more protection than threat from my father's descended figure crouching above me, which no doubt was just another example of a rather predictable "love-hate ploy" in action, as the etceteras would probably say of similar launchings and landings on that calm night in a suburb of the murderous Forties. When I slept I dreamed of melted metal and calcined faces and of flying away from it all, that is, to another ship on a flying-belt quite alone and unafraid of that future.

One day it seemed the only thing to do was to take the one pound note beneath the cut glass tray upon my mother's dressing table and convert it into brandy, lime and sodas at the nearest pub. Along the way I worked it out: the drinks were two and sixpence each and eight half-crowns made up a pound. The nearest pub was one short mile away and it was downhill going. The only thing that bothered me was stealing the pound. Yet it was then I understood one reason for stealing money: to buy oblivion with. If I could have taken only the ingredients of this potent drink from my parent's liquor cabinet I would have surely done so and knocked myself out at home. It was a day when both parents were out. But my father's liquor cabinet was the shoe space in his side of the wardrobe he shared with my mother. There he'd stowed a whisky bottle that was seventy-five percent aqua no longer vitae as I'd watered it as I'd consumed it. Apparently he'd been saving it for a binge as weeks afterwards he hit the roof but only touched me with his words.

Now I was on the downhill path to Manly which meant drunkenness as then there were five busy pubs to one small harbour town and every pub did better than good business every day and better than better every wet or dry weekend whether winter or summer. But it was mainly beer that rang the till and I was out for stronger stuff and one year under age. But ennui and other modified dissipations had given me a wan and ravaged look so that I would have passed for eighteen and had no fear of canny barmen. Barmaids I liked. The best of them combined maternal feelings with the warm bonhomie of a hostess—the worst were merely distant and efficient. Most of the barmen were morose and none were young, it being towards the end of the second world war and all the young men dead and gone or coming back in bits and pieces physically and mentally.

I'd seen a number of things that had left me out of love with life. In the window of one large Sydney bookshop were displayed to all who passed and looked photographs taken by a Japanese officer of an allied airman being beheaded by another Nip wielding a samurai sword. Opposite there were other shots, this time taken by correspondents, no doubt in the wake of MacArthur, of several Nip foot soldiers who had held hand grenades to their chests and pulled the pins out—possibly the quickest disembowellings in the east. And even the *Saturday Evening Post* in brightly coloured articles illustrated what it looked like to have a bomb explode directly in front of the human body. It quite outdid the comic strips. I think the intention was to dull what desiccate sensibilities remained after six years of legalised mass murder on all sides. The intensified reds and yellows, the subtle greys and mauves of the *Evening Post*'s detailed bodies disintegrating swifter than the already melted eye could have seen, yet caught in the lens of a specially timed camera and copied painstakingly down to the last flying shreds of khaki and flesh—and the wounded, flayed and living, half skull faces, limbs truncated, meticulous indentikits of the worse than Frankensteinian reconstructions—all seemed part of a mass acceptance of sudden and violent death.

Even the propagandist films, the absurdly understated pukka English and the equally absurdly overstated American admitted bloody death to be the one real glory. Heroes died—cowards lived, to witness death. Despite the games of childhood emulating violence I was a confirmed pacifist before I saw the word or knew the myriad rationalisations for the constant recurrence of mass murder. I understood that people kill each other singly out of passionate rage or greed or sexual insanity. It was intolerable and real. But war was demoniacal, widespread and sanely administered, and would I knew then once and for all go on in one way or another while human life existed en masse. Perhaps a war would end all war and everything else, and perhaps that may be for the betterment of things other than human. I hurried down the hill to celebrate the death of reasonable consciousness.

I stood before the lean barman and let the mixture ring its little bells and begin to anaesthetise the better part of me until at the sixth glass I had the advice given (and not unkindly) that I'd better go while I could still walk home. I couldn't but I did because the next thing I recall was sitting in the tatty lounge and methodically breaking all my beloved swing records by holding them up in my left hand and punching them hard enough to shatter them with my right fist which became bloodied in the relentless process. For thirty years I have sought to replace the shattered irreplaceable discs—the titles haunt me: James's "Jeffries Blues", Miller's "I dreamt I dwelt in Harlem", Ellington's "My heart sings", Will Bradley's "Down the road apiece" and "Jimtown blues" and something like a hundred more reduced to slightly bloodied shards. And then I must have fallen down the high back wooden stairs because somebody carried me up and put me to bed. A doctor gave me a pill to take while my parents stood around looking worried and not saying a thing. Even when I cried out about stealing the money. Apparently they realised I had begun to kill myself, and they had begun to see why, at least for a day or two afterwards.

So I then began to compose music in my head to drown out the terminal preoccupation. Not swing or jazz but interminable symphonies and sonatas. I lived then on books and music and a little food and drink. I walked out only at night and learned by heart the tree-lined streets and garden-decked frontages of houses over an area of several miles. I'd walk from eight till ten p.m. in the often balmy, often chilly dark of night when everything seemed almost at peace. The only sound my quick footsteps and the inner music that the night and I made together and offered up to the Mystery. And sometimes I'd forget the need of getting drunk again or where the next two ounces of tobacco would come from. I kept a tin of butts (as my father did) that stank like over-smoked oysters and tasted when re-rolled like urine-soaked chaff. I could not sleep unless I sucked mouthfulls of that more than acrid smoke into my lungs until my head swam and all thought was hidden.

In dreams I'd come across a girl seated in the middle of nowhere. A girl whose eyes were large and dark as gently, almost lovingly, they'd look into my own. And when she took my hands she'd speak to me of how far I had come and how much further on I would have to go before I even recognised some of my many selves enough to stop walking backwards in the two dull dimensions of my hieroglyphic sense of reality's stony wall. And when I'd wake I'd long for her and look for her in lighted doorways or through opened, glowing windows that I quickly passed at night. But surely I had seen the eyes in the adolescence ravaged face of a girl at work who'd asked to be my friend and whom I'd treated coolly, caring for another who treated me coolly, and who was treated coolly in her turn by another. Love and every other reason for existing lived in music and in writing. I would keep diaries and record my mystified reactions to the world about the rat run walls and starling lousy eaves of my home. As each fragment of awkward prose fiction was written it was burnt, and at the end of the year the diary full of cryptic compressed notes was torn up and yet another begun. The future seemed unmusical.

Dying

It seemed by the maladministrations of well meaning others one could be almost, some quite specifically, killed in point of fact. Lying at home in a deck chair, gazing up at desultory clouds and memorising Debussy's *Nuages* while doing little else; not even washing as often as usual and shaving even less—even letting the hair grow almost long when short back and sides was the style as well as the unwritten rule. In deepest winter wearing over the shabbiest trousers, shirt and sweater, an even shabbier dark overcoat a size too large for my bony, pallid frame. In summer never swimming or even visiting the beach.

The sunbathing girls and women excited and disturbed me beyond control, their languorous attitudes of half submission, half challenge, the white and brown thighs leading up to the plumpest of cotton-packaged parson's noses, the armpits shaved yet darkly shaded—an incredibly enveloping air of meltings and erections, of impossible contacts (what would one do, or rather *how*?), a breeze perfumed by or a pulsating stillness of heat drenched in the odour of sun lotions and the sweet musky sweat of health accentuated by the omnipresent salt air. I would not walk there awkwardly with an uncontrollable penis and skinny legs in ridiculously oversized khaki shorts.

Why was everything oversized? They were "passed down" from cousins, uncles, even some of my father's things. I'd had new clothes when I'd left school early to start work as a messenger-boy for a city dental warehouse at twenty-five shillings a week. I was now seventeen and still in love with Judy Garland but seemed to lack the courage to go to work. It was I suppose a natural laziness and an innate revulsion from the blindly accepted habit of compulsive servitude to work that should have been done by machines or at least a more mechanical creature than I assumed myself to be. I wanted to —what did I want myself to do? I didn't know, and that was all there was to it. In consideration I didn't particularly want to sit alone all day in a deck chair watching clouds or, in the colder weather, huddled over a book and wearing a mouldy, oversized coat. I had at least a preoccupation that was almost in fact an occupation: the tracking down at far-off suburban theatres of early Judy Garland films. I'd scrounge a shilling and walk sometimes up to four or five miles to an ageing, weathered theatre and wait in the all but empty stalls or the totally empty gallery for the badly jumping print and the almost inevitable blackout due to wornout equipment or a drunken projectionist. It all added to the comical pathos of rapidly passing youth—theirs, not mine.

I was born middle-aged and now seemed to be verging on a premature senility while my favourite male cousin had flexible muscles over the lower abdomen grown by tennis playing and no doubt frequent fucking. He was four years my senior and already married and separated. One horribly wintry morning he called and found me limp and chilled and, with the best intentions, exercised my non-existent muscles for a dreadful half-hour then threw me still limp and chilled into a tub full of cold water. I knew it was all wrong but he assured me before he left feeling much better that I would greatly benefit from the exercise and the icy immersion. I felt even more than ever like nothing on earth. By the afternoon I was uncontrollably shaking from a chill. By evening I was prone and trembling, racked by inflamed and assaulted nerves from skull to soles, a case of over-all neuritis. My mother rubbed me with warmed oil. My father gave me two ounces of his own hard-come-by tobacco which I smoked through the aeon-long, the neverending winter night; sixty thin cigarettes which dulled the penetrative pain.

Towards morning I collapsed rather than fell asleep and felt a warmth beckoning me and an almost complete cessation of pain. I was in a dark and cavernous place and heading slowly towards a point of light that was more than flame, more even than day. I knew that if I reached it I would be dead to the world and alive again. I strove towards it, yet, under the dark roof with grey and glistening walls on either side and underfoot the adamantine rock, and behind, a thousand best forgotten lives, I knew I had to wait before I could come into the sparkling lights and colours of what lay so far, so near, before me. And I woke in pain, sweating like a fountain, my heart crescendoing and drumming like a Beethovenian finale—only this I knew, it was another beginning. I knew where I had been, in the darkling cave stretching between human life and death, and that no night was black as it, no day as bright as that which lay ahead. And yet it seemed that I had chosen to remain "alive" and vulnerable among dangerous friends and worse that ticked the clock around of human intercourse.

I had and have no special love of human nature. Pity and disgust are the two emotions it stirs oftenest in me. Compassion's for the angels, hatred for the devils, to indulge in. Yet if this is the case there are no human beings in the main, only angels and devils while the remnant of the rest of us are human and unhappy to be so without wishing ever to join the majority of the world dwellers, the angelic, the diabolical. I thought then that I must be other than human, devil or angel. Not better, but different. I continued on recovering to sit and watch the clouds; to track down musicals; to read a dozen books a week. Only I almost knew that I was waiting for a purpose to exist, a raison d'être beyond the sentimental piffle of nominal work and nominal marriage and nominal parenthood.

I ventured out with my dog and roamed North Harbour's bushy slopes and little fawn coloured beaches with grey, oyster studded rocks. My dog would ecstatically roll and snuffle over dead fish and wrack at the tideline, or burst exultantly into and out of bushes that encroached and gathered about the bases of gums at the side of the pathway. We'd move together towards the last small beach and broach the ingress of herbal scented bushes and lantana clumps that covered the path onto the small plateau beneath the heights of Dobroyd. Once there we'd sit awhile, he panting with the sustained effort, preoccupied by scents or fleas or both, I cozened out of my by now habitual pessimism by a panoramic view of the harbour's heads and the utterly unlike twin attractions of all my meditations then, the town and the vast Pacific. The first began and ended at wharf and Ocean Beach by the mast-high signatures of green foliaged Norfolk Pines, and roofs of singular orange and multi-coloured tiles, of dark grey slate, of silvered over or red-leaded corrugated iron, and leading like the fulfillment of a kindly promise from wharf to beach the way of the palm-centered Corso's wide mainstreet of bright shops. The second was everywhere, before, behind, surroundingly, the great ocean's presence, the slow pulse of half the world, of blues and greens and whites beneath the genius of the sun or cloud-occulted nether tones of gall and livid greys. A beginning it was, but of such strife and hellish endurances that had I known its sequent fire and ice I might have striven towards the cave's oblivion, or that light of a changing life.

I twice tried to kill myself although never very thoroughly. The first attempt was at about the time Gandhi was killed. The broadcast news of his final act of absolving the murderer from the karma impressed me, but another interesting person had been summarily obliterated and it seemed the only thing that I could do by way of protest was to obliterate myself. I started at it in the bathroom gingerly drawing a razor blade across the wrong part of my gristly wrists. Snivelling and nicking away I managed to draw a little blood at last but it was becoming too painful and I could not make that Samurai slash for the life or death of me. I transferred to the kitchen stove, placed a small pillow inside it, turned on the gas and poked my unhappy head in, but the kitchen door was open and the window as well and after a while the smell of gas kept me wide awake and nauseated into the bargain. So I turned off the stove and crushed about ten aspirin tablets to powder and drank them with water, then went to die on the couch in the living room and fell asleep from nervous exhaustion. I slept until my parents came home and I showed them the nicked wrists and the cushion in the stove and the glass from which I'd drunk the aspirin. In a week or two it was decided I should be "treated" at Prince Alfred.

Once there I knew I was in an experimental ward and was to be given electrical shock treatment. For the first few days I was fed nothing but mashed potato. At night a little Dutch nurse came to put me to sleep with a hypodermic. It stung and I swore, and the poor little nurse so full of pity wept, and, I should imagine, was transferred. One morning at about two a.m. I was ushered trembling and terrified into a young doctor's official presence. He filled his pipe, lit it and sucked, then asked what was the matter with me. Dying for a cigarette and full of emptiness and self-pity I told him brokenly of the suicide attempt, then wept. He seemed disgusted with it all and coolly told me to go back to bed. That afternoon the lift took me swiftly up one flight to the treatment floor. I had had no lunch that day and my sideburns had been shaved off. I was to be given my first electric shock.

The wards on each floor had wired windows like a bird cage. I was left outside a room with an open window. I stood shivering not from cold. I saw a young man laid on a narrow bed surrounded by nurses while a doctor applied what looked like a pair of earphones to his head. And then he was bucking and arching upward and hissing like an angry boa constrictor, then the nurses were holding him down, laughing and yelling encouragement to each other while one began to slap his face and it was over. I was taken into the room and onto the narrow bed. I was half-conscious already but felt the sucking pressure of the wet electrodes clamp my temples which had been rubbed hard with brine solution.

Some days later I began to recall I had woken from nothingness somewhere else with a bad headache and had not known for a while just who or where I was. But every two days it was to be repeated. I remember asking a nurse why I had been left outside that open window. She explained that fear made it quicker and easier to knock the patient out. I then asked a fellow patient, a dull witted boy about my own age, how many shocks he'd had. He said he thought it was sixteen. I could not eat my mashed potato or even look at my grandfather's copy of the Collected Works of William Shakespeare. About the second week I watched through the wired windows black American soldiers billeted within the hospital grounds. They smoked Lucky Strikes. I knew the taste and sputter of saltpetre when the cigarette was lit. I met briefly once or twice a tall wan girl from another ward. She said she didn't care what happened to her as long as it was somewhere miles away from the caged-in treatment wards. I believed her. I caught her mood while overhearing a sweet Glenn Miller record playing on a radio somewhere. Another week and several blurring shocks later I was taken home.

After a month or two had passed it was decided I should be sent to Broughton Hall for further treatment. I went to stay at the Randwick home of a young chemist, the friend of my kindly ex-employer. The boss was camp and the friend was camp and apparently I was not, but apart from being shown some beach photos of oiled and buttocky boys, and told that naked I'd look as good as them I was left alone in a room surrounded by books of poetry and novels. All day I'd read and in the evening I'd drink and smoke and listen to good music with the boss and friends. Apparently my chemist host was considering a career in psychiatry and a live, morbid specimen to hand was better than a thousand books. But I was reading verse—the Georgians and the Imagists, and picking plums out of the grey pages of Penguin New Writing, "Lay your sleeping head, my love" and the tragic John Cornford's "Huesca"—was hearing the Mahler Society's recording of "The Song of the Earth" with a tiny photo of the composer's angst-ridden face on the label. "Trinkern, plaudern" was for others.

Then one night the radio announced two bombs had atomised most of two major Japanese cities and their civilian inhabitants. I had to protest though the war apparently was over, so I wrote down my first attempted poem, an angry rhyming jingle in tetrameters, and a false start. Within a day or two I found my forte lay in love lyrics so for a while I wrote of love, at least two lyrics every day. Then one wild night I drank too much SVR and pear essence and falling down the stairs broke my host's mother's favourite statue and was deposited fully dressed in a bathtub full of lukewarm water. Hearing of these misadventures my parents took me home again and from there, soberly despairing, I was sent off to Broughton Hall.

This was its old environment next door to the grimmer Callan Park. Now I was in a ward with men of varied ages and complaints. These windows, too, were wired. I held within my arms a sobbing wreck of seventy or more who must have died within a day or two if not then—the memories are warped and scattered. In a small room with twenty men I sat watching a thick, black, twitching conduit pass from a plug beneath the door, dispensing its convulsive load as one by one the twenty waiting men walked into but did not walk away from where I must go, and went in course. In several weeks I was discharged in a disorientated state, fearful above all else of "treatment". But I had begun to write again and to read more avidly than before. Poetry kept me alive within but could not cancel that despair that coloured every verse I wrote with sombre, melancholy tones. I had the friendship of a girl but wanted more than she could give and even the companion of my childhood was alienated by my deathly moods. It was as if I was reliving in a prison an interminable sentence. I had been alive, it seemed, forever and could grow no older. I was Jew Süss, the Wandering Jew and Peter Vanderdecken and Chris Brennan's lonely Nietzschean Wanderer. But now there were verses to be written and somewhere, perhaps, the true friend.

Breakthroughs

My grandmother died when I was nineteen and ready
to try and kill myself again. This time
I had a plan that had become obsessional.
I was to go and stay at my uncle's farm
where on arrival I'd borrow my cousin's rifle,
go down to the small island of rocks and trees
that grew on a flat near the creek, the burial ground,
or rather the burning place of all dead cattle,
and once there shoot myself, through the head probably—
I'd seen it work with cows, why not with humans.
My grandmother's last days had sounded terrible,
and I'd been too unwell myself to visit her
at the St Leonard's Hospital with my stricken
mother. The terminal illness was apparently
blood poisoning complicated by diabetes
melitus. A routine job of toenail trimming
by a chiropodist careless in her work
had brought on gangrene in the foot, and toes
had to be amputated eventually.
But the bad blood spread and finally clumsy
handling of her square, ungainly body
on an operating table dislocated
something within her and she began to die
miserably, yet gratefully at the end.
I had no further need to convince myself
of the recurrent obscenities of existence.
My morbidity had frightened away the few
girls I knew and even my oldest friend
was unable to cope with what had happened to me.
As well I'd developed a singular obsession
that I was Adam cursed by Brennan's Lilith—
I saw her shadow everywhere and even
the Moreton Bay Fig Trees, so benignly shading
and generously sheltering, seemed to hiss and spread

their massive dark leaved branches threateningly
over me. Some nights I was afraid
to sleep, and eating seemed a waste of effort.
But time stretched out before me like the Wanderer's
road in some perpetual grey dawn
when all my longings were of westering flights
of birds into the golden sinking sun.
So one dark evening in late autumn I
and my parents travelled south in the steam train towards
my uncle's farm. I could not talk with them
or read the paperback I'd blindly bought.
It was perhaps the longest several hours
that I recall enduring in my life.
Of our reception and the night that passed
I recall nothing—only that in the morning
I carried out my deathly plan to the point
of reaching the tiny wood with rifle and bullets,
then found I could not load the gun or had
the slightest knowledge of its simple working.
Then something about the surrounding fields and hills
caused me to overturn all thoughts of death
by suicide. In melodramatic fashion
I picked up a piece of wood shaped like a trumpet
and holding it to my mouth intoned the words
of Browning: "Dauntless the slug-horn to my lips
I set, and blew 'Childe Roland to the Dark
Tower came'."—And then for seven endless months
I worked as hard as I have ever worked,
returning lithe and wiry in the spring
to where my parents lived then, at my grandmother's.
The house had been divided into two
and the other half was rented by a young
couple. The wife was several years my senior
but she and I had in the past spent many
evenings together while her husband worked
at night. And sometimes I would baby-sit
for them. I had become fixated on
her thin and hawk-like face and filled-out body.

The slightly crazy dialogues we held
had been of music, poetry and the occult,
and she had scared us both with amateur seances.
Now I stood before her new and into manhood.
Wordlessly she ran into the house
on seeing me and left me standing there
talking embarrassedly to her sister.
I thought I had offended in some way
but later in the evening when I knocked
she answered as a friend, inviting me
to spend the remainder of the evening with her
alone, her husband working and the children
asleep. We settled on the well-known couch
within the lounge where I had crawled upon
the lifeless yet envenomed bee so many
years before, and she explained her flight
from me that afternoon. I had appeared
before her for the first time as a man
and she had been afraid of what she'd felt
towards me. Then I asked if I might kiss her.
At her assent I numbly and quite briefly
pecked at her lips. She took me in her arms
and, drawing our bodies closer, indicated
that sofas were intended to lie upon
as often as to sit, then holding my head
between her hands, her softly swelling body
pressing against and wonderfully fitting
into my own, breasts, belly and full thighs,
she told me she would teach me how to kiss.
Then for the first time in my life I felt
a mouth opening to mine and tasted another's
tongue, curling and flexing and withdrawing
against my own in passion and delight.
I learned her body like a book and lived
for kisses and caresses through the months
of spring and summer, yet collapsed again
and by the following autumn was in hospital.
But prior to this I'd met a man who for

a decade after taught me how to live
just as my neighbour's young wife cruelly and kindly,
generously, selfishly had taught me how
to love. At the hospital I witnessed a middle-aged
European die after shock treatment,
his death possibly occasioned by
brain damage received some years before
in a concentration camp. I'd gone in placidly
with copies of Eliot's *Four Quartets* and Helen
Gardner's commentary for company.
Nightly a not-unattractive nurse would lie
with me until the pheno-barbitol
dosage of oblivion was administered.
At the death of the European I rejected
all acceptance of the "treatment" and signed
myself out of the dubious environment
of mental hospitals for another fifteen
years. With the help of my friend I began to work
again in the city, to take a slightly more
positive stance towards the pursuit of love.
The years brought truth and poetry, and lies
and poetry, beauty and ugliness,
the usual opposites to be encountered
between the cradle and the springboard grave.
But now I had the one vocation
mocked at and honoured by my schizoid fellows
at one and the same time, the paradoxical art
and craft of the wise fool, the accolade
of my good and bad angels, and a willing
life sentence in the quarry of words.

The Poems

The Poems

The poems came
and when they wouldn't
come I'd find them
hiding here and
there, between the
seawall's jointures
small as a scurrying
ant or lumbering
beetle, or halfway
up a hugely
spreading pine,
a knot of resin
or a resting
pigeon, or
upon the salty
lawn between the
pines and wall
the strutting, bowing
birds themselves,
or down about
the line of wrack
dogs abounding,
sniffling blue-bottles,
chasing seagulls
grey and white,
red or black legged.
All along
the best part of
a mile of finely
sifted beach sand
grew the poems,
out of thousands
of those units
of detritus,

weathered match-sticks,
bubble weed and
cuttle shells and
timber fragments,
buttons and the
tins and bottles
of the ships' vast
thoroughfaring,
and the salty,
fatty, acrid
odour of it
all. At either
end of the curving
beach distinctive
settings: the pool
and rocks of Queenscliff,
by the pool the massive floodgates
twinned, debouching
the lagoon through
concrete tunnels
six feet high,
under the sand
for several hundred
yards they travelled
interrupted
by two funnels
rising from the
sand like towers.
There were poems
reeking from them,
sticking to the
twin-mouthed tunnels'
wave and tide slap
echoing walls.
Up and down them
roved the boys and
gamer girls,
beneath their feet

unavoidable
shells of poems,
at the lagoon end
shoals of little
fish poems. Under
the traffic and foot bridge,
about the bases
in the warmer
sandy-slushy
shallows grew the
mollusc poems
and on up the
weedy length
of brown lagoon,
poems of rushes,
arrow straight.
On the banks
the quaint screwdriver
shells and gritty
path between
the rushes and
the she-oaks, pines
and coral trees.
All about them
and above them
and upon them
grew the poems.
Dwarfed and twisted
trunks arthritic
and enduring,
elephantine;
harsh and thorny
branch fists tossing
crimson outbursts
in the solar
golden full-face;
and the green and
vulnerable

twelve inch crosses
tipping the up-
reaching pines
were poems also.

At the beach's
southern end
the coarsely sanded
little bay
of Fairy Bower.
Atop the beach
a promontory
strategically
situated
among whose clustered
trees and bushes
couples met
and offered up
to whatever
randy Eros
poems of
the coupling game.
Out of Manly's
narrow tar-seal
streets, and in them,
higher than the
bungalows'
fern-motifed
fore-tiles
and the several-
storeyed blocks of
residential
flats and pubs
and tidy shops
between the oval
and the fifty
climbing stone steps
ending Pine street

rose the hilltop
houses', sea-viewed,
terraces of
flower poems;
slatted based
and shaped verandahs
jutting into
air like ship-bows,
little towers and
turrets rising
up like stanzas
and before them
slammed together
out of sandstone
blocks a sculpted
kangaroo, a
home-made poem.
Up another
hundred feet
and back another
quarter mile,
the loveliest poem
of them all:
the crown of Red Hill
and its view,
a dozen miles
of coast and ocean.
Also on the
left the ballad
of the local
brassy-helmet
hung and crimson-
chariot centered
fire station,
and a third way
down the steep
and busy hill-road
perched upon a

pole, encircled
by a pile of
several hundred
rubber tyres,
the scarecrow-clothed
and stylite dummy,
ribald poem
of the local
tyre factory.

Above the oval's
odes of sporting
effort and the
endlessly
reiterated
narratives
of spectators
rose a wooded
area.
Here came gangs
of boys and sportive
girls and muscat
gulping drunks
to make rough poems
of the chase
or valentines
to the god of grapes.
The tram track cut
a winding course
through the rocky base
of the park's rise
(wild poems along
the fern-edged lines)
towards the summit
of Red Hill.

By the harbour front
the ferry wharf

and once between it
and the path
to Fairlight stretched
the wooden poem
of the white railed
Esplanade
beneath whose walk
the shark-proof mesh
enclosed a poem
of a pool
and glowing beach.
Then on the way
to Fairlight Pool—
halfway between
and up a hill
there was a private
hospital
where I was born—
upon that calm,
pine-shaded path
poems of lilies
grew beside,
and landward rose
fine timber homes,
far more than houses,
poems with walls
and slated roofs
that looked across
the bay towards
North Harbour's lyric
beaches and the
epic bulk
of Dobroyd Point,
while spreading out
below the path
like verses shaped
in golden stone
the pocked and rocky

pool-caesuraed
margins of
the salty shore.

The real poems
were everywhere else
than within me
and I would have to
get there somehow,
get into
the world of selves
and singular poems
of the multiple
self of selves,
the pluralistic
being of the
very place,
the whole poem
and its verses
of the place
and its personae:
things and persons
in that other-
wise of world and
microcosmic
levels of the
poems grounded
in the being
of myself and
everything.

Bucolics

Pea Picking

To realise the futility of pea-picking,
its broken-backed and bruised-kneed endurance
tested up and down the crowded rows
of squat, green, sparsely bearing bushes;
the side-of-the-finger-splitting ritual,
left and right forefingers and thumbs
cut and bruised bloody, the neck breaking
under the bludgeoning sun, the eyes, ears, nose
and lips crawling with stickybeaking flies;
the stink or perfume (sometimes vaguely both)
of your fellow pickers beside and ahead of you;
to understand why you are doing this at all
day after blistering day for four shillings
a bushel or two kerosene tins full you had to be
either seventeen and desperately
in need of more than two pounds to buy the Collected
Letters of John Keats (that is ten bushels
when you were averaging four bushels a day
for the several days allotted to the picking).
Or perhaps you had to be Aboriginal
and aged from fifteen to sixty-five (male or female)
and be able to knock off ten bushels a day,
bushes and all, when you were supposed to pick
selectively, that is to leave the younger,
smaller pods for a second picking. Or you
might have even needed to be the farmer
himself. Too busy to supervise; keeping up
with most of the Aboriginals, only picking
selectively. Up five chains of bushes
and down five chains of bushes for about
five or six aching hours a day. I say
"futility" for I was too tired each day
to read the book when I had it; the Aboriginals
spent most of their pay on headache engendering wine;

and the farmer, my uncle, always seemed to time
his pickings to coincide with a glutted market.
The whole thing was an exercise in futility.
The old hands had pads of cloth or soft leather tied
to their knees and kept their backs fairly straight.
But if you were seventeen as I was then
and uninstructed you simply agonised
on sore knees shuffling forward boustrophedon
in a more or less literal way, knee-nudging over
soft and lumpy strips of bare earth
getting to feel a tiny twig or pebble,
even the compressed soil's own modifications
and innate consistencies of texture. The bushes
themselves becoming flayers of raw thumb
and finger-pad, splitters and groovers of nails,
the plump pods' contents edible but eventually
uninviting. Something like a vestigial
competitive spirit drove one to try and at least
keep up. The dust of earth and leaf-dust crimping
the nostrils, the heat of days turning the tongue
into a strap of hide cleaving to white paste.
The crazy fantasies: would Toulouse-Lautrec
have walked on his half-length legs and have merely plucked
the bushes' burdens without even looking down?
Would the Aboriginal girl in front have underwear
beneath her sack-like skirt, or a brassiere under
the off-white shirt? No, you saw small breasts
and purple-brown nipples once, and when she saw
you looking she smiled but not invitingly.
The black folk smelt of wood smoke and leaf mould.
I had been told I would smell to them of sour milk
and rancid butter. There were several deodorants
on sale even then but none of us thought to use them.
The girls had thin legs, thin thighs, and almost all
were waistless. But their faces were like a friendly
fruit, large, dark, with rounded features full
and ripe until the faces of my own kind
soured and flattened out to thin diminished

creases, cracks and bumps. At day's end I
would go to wash and eat and sleep at the farmhouse.
The Aboriginal pickers lolled or squatted
in the big barn's earth floored musty gloom, gathering
beside the several loaned hurricane lanterns
and about the central fire of sticks on which
a frying pan sputtered blessings on eggs and bacon
and later the communal billy black
as the brew it smokily and sweetly boiled.
Aperitifs of muscat and sweet sherry
were passed from hand to hand in the habitual
surreptitious manner, and the pouches
or battered tins lay open between crossed legs,
rice paper stuck to bottom lips as coarse
tobacco was reduced to fragrant shreds
in hands still acrid with the bushes' juices.
Then soft guitar accompanied song and softer
talk and sudden swallowed shouts as someone
gulped who should have sipped. And I awake
upon a sheeted bed two hundred feet
away, aware would lie and wonder if
the younger ones would go into the night
and love, as I would have given Keats's Letters
so to do. And out across the back
verandah of the farm I'd peer into
the starlit dark—so large the distant stars—
while through the barn's gapped timber walls the lanterns
and the dull glow of the compact cooking fire
showed, even the spark-sized crimson points
of hand-rolled cigarettes would wink and almost
beckon. Now I think the only ones
to leave the barn a while went to excrete.
More privacy was needed than a darkened
cow-bail or a tree's wide bole to lure
those shyest lovers out. They slept together
in a tribal dream of tiresome work and welcome
food and memoried rest. No taboos but
commonsense and something like distaste

to elevate a white farm to the statute
of home-ground. The elder ones, perhaps, while partly
drunk may have partly scored, but when the last
birds had quietened and the only sound
was cattle foraging about the dry lawn's
dew-soaked chaff, both barn and farmhouse turned
lights down and out. And then across the cooling
fields came mistily and fragrantly
sleep to all and Alchera's dreams to some.

Hunting Birds

At first there was merely the picking off of the smallest birds
with an air rifle in my uncle's tatty orchard—
ill-kempt pear and untended apple trees that habitually,
absentmindedly gave a sort of fruit more or less
on seasonal time. But the tiny birds (name them if you can:
some blue with red, some brown, some dusty grey all over)
would occasionally topple and plummet to iron-hard earth
and twig-disordered grass like wrongly coloured shuttlecocks,
about that big, that small. Their tiny polls or breasts
bloodied and I would wonder what the hell to do
with them till farm cats took to following me. One day
I nearly gelded myself carelessly cocking the gun:
the lever slipped from my careless hand and snapped shut against
the stock where I had it braced high between my legs.
I limped away from the orchard with blood-blistered inner thigh
and bruised testicles vowing never to shoot another
bird. Clearly the bird god had struck in a minatory rather
than terminal fashion. Then years later as hoarse voiced sub-
adolescents, my country cousin and partner in many crimes
(some tender and personal) and I would penetrate
the high creeper and branch hung glooms of a mountain creek-bed,
making noises like mating doves or wood pigeons,
"Woo-woo! Woo-woo!" with a throaty chirruping variation
thrown in aphrodisiacally. Then when the duller among
the love-lorn lonelies came to meet their demon lovers
we'd bounce catapulted pebbles off their already addled
pates and breast-bones, all of which were so soundly constructed
not one fell but with a squirt of bird shit and a
wild chirring of wings (and doubtless a bruise or two)
they'd escape from us. Though one day I missed a pigeon and brained
one of my tiny, earlier would-be victims—Ah god,
the feel of the match-stick neck, the still warm, soft breast feathers
and their underlying talcum of white dust, the cold wire
of the little claws. The chill sank deeper and was again melted.

The last time I hunted to kill was some years later than this
and nearer to manhood. My cousin and I knelt down behind
a dead log and sighted with our pea-rifles something like
a challenge. We lined up one big hawk, maybe an eagle,
surely a wingspan of five feet, something that preyed on and tore
the livers living out of poor defenceless rabbits
that we shot, trapped or garrotted, sometimes with the use
of stinking demoniacal ferrets. This big-shot bird
was taking it easy sixty feet away on a dead branch
thirty feet high with a backing of blue air and white cumulus.
Something already had died, something better had grown
in its place in my psyche. But my cousin and I crouched low,
fingers to lips, then curled compressing triggers and the
first bullets flew, the sudden concussions of noise cracking back.
The big bird sat on aloofly. In growing pique, then anger,
then hatred of that feathered dignity, we told
ourselves its curved beak still was red-brown with old blood
of lesser, gentler lives, still tiny blebs of flesh
adhering that the dry as death branch had not wiped clean.
The hawk—for hawk it was—twitched its head to left and right
at the flat concussions of unexpected rifle fire.
And then began the contest. Whether that bird was unwell
and could not clear out with one swoop of wings or whether it had
seen us and so despised the crouching groundlings with their
insults, heavy as misaimed lead, we'd never know.
I think now a maestro of the southern skies had chosen
to take rest between large flights towards the riper denizens
of earth and rarer haunts of high rock-face on the seamed
and frontal features of the mountain we called our own.
That bird knew, and overlooked, its natural yet
unimportant enemies: this time two partly
adult human males with their lethal pin-pricking
and innocuously named pea-rifles, shooting wide.
Then my cousin hit a wing and I another part
of that heroic, savage entity and it fell,
then partly flew, flapped and fluttered down past
and below us, onto a small rock centering a pond of the creek
of deep blue sky reflecting water, and perched square

in full sighting view upon the rock, closer
than before. We emptied a box of bullets into the pool
and at the hawk. Then we began to hit, and as
it died it flexed its massy wings and launched upon
the bloodied dark of water, and we slowly climbed
down to the unquiet pool, all our frenetic joy
of the hunt gone sour in us, even in my callous cousin.
As for me, the first tangible guilt of my life
embodied itself there in the water-crucified hawk.
We fished the surprisingly smallish body out—twelve inches
in sodden length with a wing-spread of maybe three feet, a decent,
everyday, feathered forager and scavenger.
So shrunken in such absurd, unnecessary death
that then and there I made a vow to kill no more
in "sport" anything that moved or flew or swam
upon the beastly and the beautiful terrene surface
that I and my cousin infected with our lethal presences.
But we both, after hiding the dead bird, boasted loud if not
too long upon a major kill. He went to use up
cartridges upon the pretty rodents (he was
selling skins) while I returned to sulk and sear
and merge with prematurely grey Alastor on
a mountain ledge—among the copies of the *Farmer's*
Gazette, the *Bulletin Reciter*, one tattered *Chums*,
and Lawson and the Banjo was one *Collected Shelley*.
Now I was and am a Keats man; rarely do the followers
of either poet meet rewardingly; as Byron
or Wordsworth aficionados only when mature
can talk together. But I grew grey and cold and open
to the agonies of earth and all its living burden
a little while that far-off day, the last I hunted
living things inedible, or joyed in the kill.

Silo Treading

At silo filling time the air was similarly wet
between the dense-packed, leaf-clustered corn rows, in the little
shed that housed the howling, belting, stalk-chopping silage-
making machine and in the empty silo, treading under
a rain of moist fragments the corn leaves, corn stalks, stray cobs
into a green pudding that would cook itself, beginning
the thermic process even while we trod that upright vintage.
But the whole process depended on corn. And corn is a truly magic
thing. As much a gift from the gods as the grape. It shares with the grape
religious rites and its history is linked with the dismembering
and rebirth of a god. I was nearly partially dismembered myself
one season, hacking at heavy stalks and zipping swiftly upwards
with a saw-bladed reaping hook. It slipped from my grasp in my sweat-
slippery hand
and I mechanically hauled at it stuck in the base of a stalk and tore
a half inch gash in my second finger, nearly lifting off
the top of it, only the bone and the nail held things together until
about forty-eight hours had passed and my relatives said they needed more
help.
But sometimes there was the picking of the fruit of the corn. I dimly
remember as a child it must have been picked in its husk because
there would be at the appropriate time get-togethers of neighbouring
families
after tea and late into the night for little boys and girls.
After the fiendish games of pursuing the nesting mice to their deaths
from the barn's cornerfuls of unhusked corn we would at first
with enthusiasm gradually turned into lethargy run the finger
taloned with leatherheld three inch nail down the harsh cocoon
of the husk to disclose the gold, the betel-red, the milk-white grains,
until someone would carry us snoozing into a shadowy corner on top of
more corn (and mice) and fulsome sacks of sweet and foul smelling
mixtures
of things that only adults understood the use of. But in
the later years my uncle husked the cobs on the standing stalk

and fed them to the cattle as an additive or prelude
to the plum-pudding silage that the cows went crazy over, screaming
like overweight adolescent girls to get at it as though
it were some edible pop-performer, another dismembered god
and would roll their eyes and bony hips and bump the stalls and belch
and shit while gorging. Cows are unmentionably crass and canny
at the same time. Bulls are bulls—that is, you keep out of their way
in and out of serving times. Sometimes they sing in Brahmsian
monotones, sometimes they shriek and kick up clods, sometimes
they even rupture their pizzles masturbating into a grassy
mound. But only cows really care for them. And only
they really care for cows as cows despite the farmer's habitual
endearments and namings. But corn—or the stalks thereof—and the
sandpaper raspy
leaves. And the thick, wet air between the neverending rows.
One humid day after several hours of hacking, humping and dumping
those full green six feet and more stalks I fell down dead asleep
in a chocolate furrow and did not dream of anything for the first
and last time in my life. When I awoke an hour later
my disgusted cousin was half a dozen rows on having left mine
like gapped teeth in between. However, my uncle even stopped letting
the cobs grow on the green stalks and soon it was cut and hack
and stack on the sled and chop and stamp down, and that was it.
The neighbour's son upheld the Attis myth in the form of adding
three severed fingers to the silage pudding. Those machines
were gluttonous for everything choppable. But while there was
the neighbour's mutilated son, there were also the neighbour's
daughters to help stamp down the silage and in between loads there were
sessions of mutual inspection. Then, one sad afternoon
the good share-farmer's better daughter, sweet Laura of the warm,
wide face and narrow hips and feet like pizza plates came shyly
up to me as I stamped on and on under a shower of fragrant,
tickling chips and looked at me from the ladder top and spoke
with eyes as large as curiosity, and I nodded, thinking
she was offering maximum assistance with her remarkably functional
feet, not knowing both of us may have been blessedly released
from virginity's yoke. So we glumly trod. And I kept wondering why
she looked and looked with sadder and sadder, if not wiser, blue eyes

towards me. And as I'd shrug heaps of the wet green chips from my
shoulders she'd briefly
smile, and then there was a welcome pause and as I rolled
a cigarette with far from trembling hands she slowly crossed
without a word to the ladder, leaving as silently as she came.
And that no doubt is why her eldest child is one or two years
younger than it might have been. Then the roar and green rush
of relentless ensilage in the making all but drowned my donkey-
at-the-water-wheel treading, till I prayed like some mad catherine-
wheeling
anchorite those masochistic prayers of pious-randy
youth, and trod and trod the green wheel of the neverending
hours, stained green and yellow, smelling like a sweaty stalk,
talking and singing songs of food and drink and love to myself
in the most innocuous words ever disassembled, the cowboy tunes
of the Thirties and Forties: "San Antonio Rose", "You Are My Sunshine",
"Be Honest With Me", "I'm Walkin the Floor Over You", "Goodbye
Little Darlin",
"Old Shep", "Cool Water"—delirious with weariness and love
unsatisfied while the Niagara of shredded stalks descended
upon my cropped head, down my neck, inside my khaki shirt,
even into my underpants. Deluged with god, the blood
and semen of the cornstalk deity, I trod and chanted,
always ascending like an apprentice shaman towards that last
hole in the concrete roof from whence I'd issue on leaf-green wings
and tread upon the air up to the glazed galactophil-
ideal heaven of Khamaduk, the celestial bovine with ever-
flowing teats and other accommodations—for bulls. Back to
the heavy-footed, the Frankensteinian monster's tread, Boris's
bandy, soulful plod. In several months we'd shovel off
the top muck and the chooks would gobble it, a solid cross
between Drambuie and mud, and lurch and flap drunkenly for
a few days. Then the silage would be ready. And ploughing begin.

Herding Cows

At gut-rumbling five a.m. summer or winter
and every dark or wan pre-dawn between
stumbling into sweat-stiff shirt and stand-up trousers
that could not be folded, socks like dried-out moss,
dung and loam caked boots; feeling a way
to the lantern-lit kitchen where the primus hummed
and hissed a blue-orange flame under a kettle;
where stood the patriarch with tea and biscuits
(those crumbling brown segments of processed blotting paper
sweetened with saccharine). Two cups, four biscuits. Out.
Out into what and where on a spiteful hack
in search of what hidden and partially camouflaged creatures
and their awkward sisters and female offspring, cows.
Large moving things that ruminate and from which
milk is extracted, forcibly. The final
challenge to Women's Liberation. Big brutes
with sex like sink plungers, who took three feet
of bull and bull's essence with a spine arched high
like the Sydney Harbour Bridge, but never stopped chewing.
Mothers all womb and boot leather with God knows
how many stomachs to fill and empty. Once
I thought it was only two but when a fast train
hits a cow side on you can find chaffed grass
for nearly ten chains of track. They have emotions:
sometimes the sight or smell of blood or a strange coloured
sister disturbs them. But this isn't solely about cows.
This is about the searching for them at five a.m.
and three p.m. seven days a week on a hack
that abruptly stops on a cattle track with a thirty feet
drop onto rocks (and cow dung) to the left,
a bramble bush at eye height to the right;
who swiftly turns its narrow bony head
to bite blood bruises through the toughest trousers,
lumps out of bare legs, always about the knee,

close to its innate hateful pun, the reins
of man or boy. I have talked to my enlightenment
with animal lovers—some of my best acquaintances
etcetera—but lovers of horses and cattle
despite their differing sexes are all John Waynes.
If I forgot where I was for a moment's moment
at dawn or afternoon in search of cows—
if, say, I had in heart and mind a sonnet
to a girl with a face like the best of promises kept
three farms away, or another with a backside
like two ripe sugar melons—or if I pondered
the structure of a triolet or pantoum
or of even challenging Auden at sestinas
at five million paces—for that transcendental
moment I'd be elevated literally
to land on hard and actual ground with that arse-hole
of a horse moving on, but not one whit the faster.
We came to terms, if it shied or bit I kicked;
if it kicked I bit the bastard's hairy neck.
We were almost lovers.
The track that led from the barns
to the topmost grazing areas was straight up
or seemed so. A part of the farm was perpendicular
rising from flats and grassy hillside ground
to a razorback of rock and tussock grass
and ubiquitous fern, green fern with brown leaves, brown
fern with green leaves, green on green and brown
on brown, each spiny stem the guarantor
of a brush hook's blunting or a blistered palm.
This smallish farm was rented from his neighbour
by my impoverished uncle, already stricken
with petit mal long euphemised as "turns"
The lessee was a small and bony widow
with a profile like an active cash register
or an original model Remington typewriter.
Actually she looked like Margaret Hamilton
who played the Wicked Witch in *The Wizard of Oz*,
but I liked Margaret Hamilton who had a ghoulish

brio, whereas the widow had my uncle
by his economic balls. Yet to do her justice
she didn't really seem to enjoy it at all.
I'm older though not wiser than she was then
and think that had my uncle been otherwise
than he was, a domestically unadventurous man,
the angular widow may on occasion have helped
out with the seed pea bills, may even have paid
the subscription of the perennially unread
Farmer's Gazette. There must have been some hundreds
of unopened copies of the *Gazette* in the farmhouse
bulking out bookshelves, dropping out of drawers
and wardrobes, stuffed lumpily under the settee's mattress,
propping uneven legs of chairs and tables,
even sometimes with the David Jones' catalogue
hung on the dunny wall—but even there
though "rudely forc'd" it went unread unlike
the beautiful ads for corsetry and brassieres
and occasionally toys and always books in the sumptuous
catalogues.
But halfway up that cow track
that led to the spine that led to the mountain's base
was only halfway up to the god and devil damned
cows who liked to be on top for once
at least twice a day. Yet there were exceptions:
the jersey that I never had to tie
so gentle and so prettily endowed
with silken coat and udder always full,
who never shat or pissed in my pail or on me,
who never had a name other than Darling.
And the huge red hulk with teats like wax bananas,
impossible to milk but easy to like,
so gentle-stoical, and several others
with names that I once knew—not Dad and Dave names
like Strawb or Daisy, but Evelline and Big Tits.
When the schizophrenic centaur that was me
and the equine object that shall go unnamed
got within hearing distance of the cows'

continual champing I would call softly, hanging on
to that apocalyptic beast, C'mon,
C'mon, Ho-on, Ho-on, and other traditional
incomprehensible noises like the cries
of city newspaper boys and railway guards.
And those crates of bone and leather and grass halfway
to milk would creak and lumber upright, filing
past me, champing, out of step or stumbling
a little on a big pebble, one or two giving
a muffled moo that surely said "Keep out of
the way of Shit Head's heels" as back to the bails
we went. It was like that, a neverending conflict
between the cows, the horse and my misplaced self.
One of the imponderables of farm life
that neither I nor the animals could accept.

Country Dances

At country dances then the dead moved and jigged
with the living. These were the Saturday Night Functions at
the minuscule School of Arts in a southern valley of
the Shoalhaven in the Cinesound, Bradman, Kingsford Smith
and Pyjama Girl haunted vivid, faded, Nineteen Thirties
when the Depression was so real nobody talked
about it in front of country kids and their city cousins.
But at Saturday night dances the living lived and the dead
were kindly to us in a cobwebby sort of way.
The preparations for dancing, proper and improper
(and that only meant where a hand easily slid to and for
how long) began in the early evening when the stars
appeared. The stiff young farming men in their stiff, wide, blue
serge trousers and waistcoats would move laconically up and down
the little hall's floor, gum timber one supposes, everything
was resinous inside the hall. Outside, the sweet night
waited, full of somnolent horses, cooling Whippets
like overlarge bathtubs on wire-spoked wheels, and trimmer Fords.
Everywhere were munching, drooling, snoozing cattle
and hunting farm cats hot on the scuts of succulent rabbits.
The dogs full of veal or scraps would be lying about yawning
and occasionally farting foully up at their quaint blue-black
and pink-white garbed wards until kicked out into
the lantern mellowed entrances. But before anything
started, before the matrons came with "plates" and daughters,
the young men and one or two kids would move across the floor
shaving candlestick parings of white waxen grease
over the dancing area. Then all would skate
and slide and stamp a weird white corroboree until
the floor was "right", that is, so dangerous to move on
only the young would venture out upon that wax-white
sea at first, for later on the middle-aged
and elderly would compensate with scatterings
of sawdust, tramping up and down in strange quadrilles

while the young vainly implored the staid accordionist
or pianist or both to try and simulate
a Slow or Quick Fox Trot, a Gipsy Tap, or something
more exotic called the Veleta. There were these dances
with variations and something like a waltz. The rest
were simply barn dances. Whatever happened to
the Charleston was a social-historian's mystery.
I never saw or heard one outside my mother's suburban
kitchen at daring moments. But at those country dances
the dead were there, the local deceased. Not in the little
hall unless in eyes and shrunken backs of necks.
They stayed outside with the twitching dogs, just near the doorways'
shallows of light: at the front the ceremonial ones,
the big speakers at functions and their spouses, the fabled
cake makers and mothers of mothers, and savers of men
from themselves. While at the rear exit, near the dunnies, the still
randy old spectres, the coins-in-pocket rattlers, the denture
shifting, ever hopeful hungry ones, and those strange
old spectral girls, "notorious" and said to have had
"bold eyes" and walk "provokingly" with assertive "bosoms",
and the rest whether plump or slim, to the fore and the rear. And some
less sure, the lads and lasses who would never grow old,
wanting to come inside, not wanting to come inside.
The wild girls now were rangy, thin as not, heads capped
with home perms, lips blood-red, and most a little wobbly
on high heels. But O the stifled screams of pleasure parting
the thickest texture of the music at about ten
p.m. when I and my contemporaries had drowsily
given up trying to follow the satyrs and their future
wives or mistresses into the dark. Then supper, for which
both our heavy-lidded eyes and avid mouths
had remained open, swiftly would be served, with fruit
punch (some of which packed the same and some of which didn't).
And the plates of cakes and sandwiches, so richly varied,
so fresh and tempting, would melt and vanish into those adult
interiors. We'd be lucky to grab four sandwiches,
two fairy cakes and one crumpled slice of passionfruit cream
sponge. But there were compensations: the occasional nip

of O.P. rum from some farmer's son or hired hand
already drunk or well on the way. A teaspoonful
sufficed to fill the cooling night with sky-rocketing stars
and the sweat and cologne reeking hall with plenitude
of goodwill. Sometimes the boys were forced to dance with reluctant,
skinny younger daughters who already dreamed of
dancing with the tall young bachelor farmers, brothers
of their best friends, and not us boys, their scruffy familiars
to whom already on that or another Saturday morning
in a dry creek bed they had shown their "things" in honest swapping.
The dead were dancing then, and in a lively measure.
No sarabandes for them. Those olden shades were jigging
and tramping about, but soundlessly, among the dogs
the parked cars and tethered horses. Sometimes a dog
would stretch and yawningly exercise its salivatory
apparatus, snap at a moth fluttering singed
from some frantic ecstasy of dance about a lantern
or look up at its owners and sigh at such benign
damnfoolery. Sometimes a horse would start and almost remember
something. Occasionally the autos' isinglass windows
would click, tautening in the ever-cooling late
night air, but that had nothing to do with memory. Then,
about midnight or a little after when the elders
remembered that milking was a matter of hours away,
the function would cease to function and most of the weary dancers
would head for home and bedstead. I and my cousins would be
already snoring in the back of the icily upholstered
Whippet, our warm child bodies tucked together by tolerant
elders. And the insatiable dead would go on dancing
vaguely, and the living lovers would shriek and guffaw
until dawn's inevitable milking and the making of porridge.

Ploughing and Swearing

This was the first farmland and house that ever I knew. It was my uncle's
second or third venture into independence which in his case
meant being responsible for a small family, a small farm with large hills
always to be paid for or maybe bartered over and nearly always
an eighty hours long working week to be encountered, endured, even
at times I believe enjoyed, especially when he was ploughing a small field,
maybe one and a bit acres cupped in the brown palm of the hills'
hand up from the flats that stretched away to the river's rim. He'd think
himself unheard at that distance, nearly a quarter mile from the farmhouse,
but the cupping hills' natural amphitheatre had the very best acoustics
in the whole countryside around and my cousins and I would sometimes hear him
roaring curses while he ploughed, rolling out those incredible swearwords
like magnificent, obscene psalms to the many gods and goddesses
of intractable earth and rainless sky and the laziest team of draught-horses under
Capricorn. While from the kitchen came the cries of disapproval
from my aunt and whomever feminine guest of the morning. Always someone,
for this farmhouse was the Flats' Post Office and had installed
directly on the front verandah beside the door, a vestibule furnished
with wooden shelves and drawers and a counter that could be easily raised and lowered.
And in the drawers were postage stamps and sealing wax in red stick-lengths
and all manner of gum-backed duty seals. And on the shelves were brown paper
parcels and bundles of white and brown and especial windowed envelopes.
And there were also great and richly coloured Film Posters to paste
on the vestibule's outer walls (such posters as now the unwise pay unwisely for)
and on the posters were the remarkable profiles of Gable, Tracy and Harlow,
The Marx and Ritz Brothers, Laurel and Hardy, George Formby and once the beautiful
Jeanette MacDonald whose gently smouldering eyes and vivid mouth and long,

shapely neck gave me a small boy's erection. And lo! there was also to see in the vestibule
a large and ugly machine of many parts that typed and rang a bell
to signify the dropping of a line or possibly its displeasure.
But outside the office on the verandah, listening to my uncle's great
vocabulary of foul phrases and the shocked cries of concern
and apologies we memorised the mighty and imponderable
words and practised them at school and if overheard by the tall bee-keeping
teacher in his grey dust coat were caned before our sniggering peers.
But one bright mid-week afternoon at sandwich-munching lunch hour we stood
with a dozen schoolmates, boys and girls, watching from the hillside playground
below us the oldest draught stallion of the Flats' half-dozen farms
very awkwardly and very heriocally serving a fairly young draught mare,
his gargantuan efforts causing him to neigh tremendously loud and long
with each penetrative plunge into that more than nubile and highly appreciative
mare. And with each mighty cry reverberating sonorously
across the paddocks and up to the schoolyard witnesses a spontaneous cheer
went up and with it (well hidden in the noise) we chanted my uncle's magical
swearwords so that even sandwiches and apples were momentarily
forgotten while thankfully the pedant tended his restless bees or ate
at his nearby house a luncheon of honey sandwiches. His two unattractive
daughters were watching with us and later that afternoon on the pretence
of searching out the amber lumps of chewable gum that burst from the trunks
of some unidentifiable trees my male cousin and I played draught horses
with the partly co-operative schoolteacher's daughters. Unpenetratively
we mounted them fully dressed and then they mounted us, but it soon palled
and my moody cousin and I left the girls and went in search of the two sons
of the Pommy migrant who drove the truck that delivered the mail and picked up the milk.
The fair-haired boys were on friendly terms with us and affectionate towards each other
in a way that inspired my lazily quarrelsome cousin and I to emulate.
The elder brother led us confidingly along the shallowly watered creek bed
to where they had constructed a dam and village of rounded river stones,
mud and match sticks. It was crude, uncomplicated, but fascinating.

It made us all feel like giants officiating at the origins
of human communal life. Each day for an everlasting week we returned
to the miniature dam and its village of match huts and stockades, of tiny invisible humans
and their domesticated herds. We gave them fields and fortifications
in the overhanging creek bank, grey soil held together by grass
and tree roots and the smooth round stones. We became almost civilised
and helped each other help our microcosmic and invisible charges.
We spoke softly and chanted our songs above the original and eternal
village. Our game of making would last forever. Then one day returning
we found only the wreckage of it all. Another envious giant
had come upon our making and destroyed it. Then we all fell out
and quarrelling blamed upon each other pair the destruction of what had been
a world. Each couple accused the other of secretly returning and grossly
ravaging the sight. We struck out, backing in opposite directions
along the creek bed, throwing mud and stones and my uncle's swearwords to and
fro, shrunken to quarrelling children. Another week went by and a semblance
of amity was assumed but they were bloody Poms and we were Aussies
and nevermore would we build and play together because . . . . My cousin and I
half-heartedly tried to construct another dam and village but took to bombing
everything we built with river rocks. We let his sister officiate
at other, more fanciful, rituals in her green glen of maiden hair fern.
There we danced and wore her woven wreaths of leafage, garlands of clover.
There for a while she taught us to rebelieve in fay, and even more,
in the divine lady's perennial magic—magic of Isis, Sophia,
Mary, Kuan Yin—all the names I didn't know then yet fully believed in.
But she gentled our bellicose beings and let us play our clumsy sexual games
with ceremonial joy instead of guilty frenetics. And we would sit
together on the dry-air-wafted verandah and hear my uncle who was
their father in stentorian tones blessing and cursing his joy and bane,
the forever unco-operative and utterly dependable team.

Birds and Beasts

At my first farm up from the river flat
behind the lavatory grew the Buddleia Bush.
It seemed then as large as the house itself
and appeared to cover the same amount of ground
with the densest growth of light coloured foliage
that climbed on trunks and branches thick as saplings
at least twelve feet above our small boys' heads
and blocked all entry from the very ground up
except where hens made nests and hatched out chickens
fluffing out their feathers, flaring and pecking
at us as marauders or eerily underlining
their broodily concentrated sittings by a
muted almost ventriloqual cry of
warning that seemed to make the Buddleia Bush
extend above our crouched and interloping
selves great wings of greyish green menace.
Sometimes a disappointed hen would leave
spoiled eggs and I would carry them gently to
the place that held the greatest fascination,
half-affection, half-revulsion for me:
the pig pen, the crudest structure I had seen;
a grey fence-posted quadrangle quarter roofed
with more old timber, one long scooped out log
to feed from, the whole floored with mud and pig muck.
If there were young they'd roam between the fence gaps
and start, and wheeze and squeal at my approach,
then come back grunting their curiosity.
The boar and sows would raise their matted heads,
snouts twitching as I stood upon a railing.
Then, at the sight of eggs, would lumber up
and come forward grunting expectantly.
I'd place the rotten eggs within their yard
and each would take one, deft as connoisseurs,
rolling the egg from side to side in their mouths

until the crunch would come and their tiny eyes
would stare, then roll in ecstasies of tasting.
I knew that sometimes they would eat their children
and once was terrifyingly pursued
by an hysterical sow with yellow fangs
and slavering mouth. I would not visit them
for many days but then the fascination
would reassert and I would scout for eggs.
Each visit to them left me with flea bites.
Beside the pen an olden copper pot
stood filled with curdling milk, its cheesy smell
a part of that discordant and olfactory
octave that seemed to begin and end with cow turds.
Fresh cattle droppings and the grass and earth,
urine and milk, corn grain and bran and pollard,
the sweat of horses and their feeding bags'
hay and hessian smell. Smell of wet dog
or rabbit-gorging cat, damp snuffy smell
of newborn kittens, nose tickle of chicks.
And sights enough to glut the hungriest eyes:
bantams and guinea hens forever clucking,
beheaded roosters flapping in the bloodied
chips and sawdust by the chopping block,
the beak of the severed head still opening and closing.
Finger suckling a calf, feeling it butt
the swashing bucket, then finding it on the morrow
dead beside the cow-path, watching it melt
over days and weeks back into the earth
till only earth remained and a frame of bone.
Racing and leaping with the family dogs
through paddocks of young corn, the dogs rising
in measured jumps like hairy dolphins, reverting
to an instinctual pattern of hunting actions.
One black and tan dog's name was Mangold Wurzel—
Mang for short—who lived to a great and hoary
age. Two cats had memorable names and natures,
soft grey Marilla, charcoal black Rasputin.
Their brief years overlapped our growing days

so that they seemed to have been always there
before our coming and would ignore our going
though somehow part of the human family, more so
than the horses, cattle and birds; they were already
fictions as strange as truth and minor legends.
The incredible noisome longeurs of the milkings,
though one tried to make a ceremony of shovelling
muck, bailing up cows and wetting their teats
with a dampened cloth. But there was the almost occult,
alchemical ritual of the cream separator,
its slow-cranked whining and the eventual twin
streams of its metamorphosed milk hypnotically
flowing before our fixated eyes. This was
when cows were milked by hand and a magic machine
like the separator seemed almost above
the business of filling buckets with white froth.
My cousin showed me his wrists which were at least
half an inch wider than mine and flexed the muscles
at the base of left and right hands' thumb and forefinger
as though it were a sign of initiation.
And the lives of his parents seemed innate with rhythms
that entranced rather than activated my own
emulation. Watching my aunt who was
my father's sister making butter: the steady
beating and whipping accompanied by her slightly
nasal and high-pitched humming of a tune,
and at the same time a preoccupied chewing
softly of her own tongue in her cheek,
a flexing of the jaw—familial traits
that both my father and I, too, as I grew older
would practise unconsciously—then the final actions
of the process, patting and shaping the orange-yellow
oblong of butter sweetly sour and rich.
In that first farmhouse there were books of verse
that my genial yet plodding uncle memorised.
Out of the *Bulletin Reciter* he culled
favourites that I came partly to know by heart:
"A Bush Christening", "How McDougall Topped

the Score". But hid among these drolleri
I found the strangest poem Shaw Nielson rote,
"Marian's Child", and I pondered long on the burying
of a baby (how did it die?) in a garden late
at night. But above all these in my estimation
was a dusty and tattered volume of *Chums Annual*
already twice as old as myself. Its pictures
of hellishly threatening pirates and a dwarf
named Jethro Blink who blew poisoned darts
at schoolboys in a long and complicated
serial by Captain or Major Somebody
or Other dazzled me for hours at a time
and held my childish attention even more so
than the cream separator and my aunt's
rites of butter-making. *Chums* was my cousin's
treasure and he would supervise my sharing
of it, but generously enough. Among
the folk and their menage of beasts and pets and books
I felt at home. But it was still the living
and dying land about us made me dream
the longest and the deepest. And it was
the river and its always for me unreachable
farther bank and above, the grey bastions
of ancient rock that I kept coming back to.

The Troubled Ascent

Climbing alone the hill near the farm to get away from it all:
the adoptive feeling, the not-quite-belonging to other than one's own
family, even the inescapable drudgery of farm work,
the unavoidable cruelties of human to human, human
to animal, and the awful accommodations of the animals
to their own, the dinning roar of slow grinding hours of almost
silence overwhelming the treadmill's labouring, sunstruck prisoner.
The need for more than sleep, for something close to the spirit of music
to carry one on its Saint Christopher's back across the always flowing,
ever-changing Herakleitian stream of the hours—So on
up into the foothills on a fine Sunday morning
and thence to the base of the steepest, greenest ascent that rose no more
than six or seven hundred feet up under a jutting rock-face,
and above that a plateau of high trees and unexplorable bush.
Only a skilled climber could have scaled that overhang
of eon-weathered rock, the hill's dark bony forehead.
If I could reach the bank beneath this I would be content
to be that far above and beyond the others, the beasts, the paddocks
that had to be laboriously opened like reluctant
giantesses to be fertilised, demanding our continual
wooing, and the godlike overbearing weather's, then hugely,
prodigiously giving birth again under our constant sweating
administrations. Everything and every single being
laboured or was in labour, the diurnal, the seasonal act of
bringing to birth and dying off, the vast sexual entity
of the immediate earth, the gnomic itch in our own genitals
to ejaculate into another walking piece of earth like ourselves,
the adolescent's inadequate or insufficiently shared
sexual games, the mysterious melancholy aftermath.
The fantasies of finding another one really wanted to be with
in this and barely imagined yet sorely hungered for ways.
So to begin at the hill's chin and climb up its handsomely rotund
cheek to a nostril and rest there, breathing heavily under a lemon
tree that held bitter-sweet and knobbly yellow fruit and impressive

thorns two inches long that pierced and drew blood from careless fingers.
But the sweet and sour juice from the lemon's fruit and the higher air
were bread and wine to my resting self. And wasn't the climbing yet
another labour, a toiling away from toil towards what? A view
perhaps. But I was barely halfway up the hill's face
and would only look back and out from beneath its eyebrow; would become
the hill's human eye myself, as small as a foreign fleck
in its green iris. Climb on then, fortified by fresher air
and lemon juice. The great grey brow loomingly frowned down
not upon me but upon the Sunday lazy land below
and the mountaineer cows that stood firm in tracks no more than twelve inches wide
and cropped grass sweeter than that below and barely looked munching up at
the inevitable two-legged thorn in their leather-sided content.
Already I could inwardly hear on the lightly felt wind's breath
my song of songs of the earth and sky and ocean not far away,
and the organ chords of the rock's concentred intellect above me
parsing and analysing, mathematically summating,
rigorously indrawing and sweating out in beads of moss
the angelic zenith hymning noon. There rose up as I reached
the ledge beneath the brow a chorale of the sun and rain loving landscape
below me now of green-brown sleeping-waking paddocks of far-
reaching farms, for several miles ahead, under the skirling
windblown wreaths of cloud choristers, and beyond the miles of
many-coloured farms and steely windings of creek and barely
wider river, beyond the silver glint of township the bone-white
strips of beach, the sky-wide meeting, mating symphony
of opalescent blue and green sea stretching forever, forever
returning to me there in the glint of the hill's noon blinking eye.
The song of myself and ocean walking together along the strand
of my childhood far away from farms and their beautiful, hideous strengths,
their never mentioned weaknesses. And I stood letting the endless
music of the earth, air, ocean play its passage widely
and exquisitely through me there, a human instrument of the elements
and the mystery beyond them always and forever. There is no way
to tell you of the music that I heard then save through the medium
of music itself and I am a word merchant. If I tell you

I was renewed by sound and sight in that order, in the order
of the being of these verses perhaps it is sight that should come first—
but you will surely sense among the word-pictured sights the sounds
their souls' celebrating made, blown back to me there in wave upon wave
on the green-blue-golden vibrant strings of the wind's long reaching hair.
I was with my innermost self of selves and stayed there only long
enough to witness that music, hear that landscape sing of itself
and everything like and unlike itself (for the song's reach was generous),
and then there began the even more laborious descent
into the heavier air and banal levels of long-pig talk
and doings, down, down into the world of the corned beef luncheon,
of honest enough and filling food that helped one forget the music
but not the years unending of unread *Farmer's Gazettes* and sadder
the truncated lives of my foster parents and cousin. A week later
without the sky's music but with my uncle I crouched for shelter
under a rain-beaten log and heard his hardwon praise and that, too,
was music to my chapped ears. A good and loving-kind man,
grey by then, of my own birth sign and stricken by its accursed
blessings. Yet how sweet his modest words of praise were to me
then, and how helpfully they came though I was very near
to self-extinction or worse, self-inundation. Under the sheltering
log we crouched and made a modest covenant. I told
my gratitude, but quietly under the rain's dulling sound.
I hope he heard me. It took much effort and more than good intentions
to win his praise. I had two fathers, both hard pressed by life;
loving, flawed men. Both live on for me because they gave
much to me, modestly, shyly then—and sometimes grabbed it back.
The olden mountain range still bulks and spreads its plateaux under
a similar sun, similar rain, and I see myself alone
on a fine seventh day, hearing its other than human music.

But why did one need to get away from anything or anybody? To say there was a darker side to the far-off sunlit, rain-drenched days, the moon and star-white or occulted nights of frost or musky breezes, is not to even hint at the blocks, the alienations largely I thought were inward and my own "faults", but later to re-align with lack-love or even jealousies on the part of others, older and younger.

I tried to give, in work and company, allegiances that were not wanted, were something of an embarrassment. To have done what would have satisfied all, except myself, would have been to remain inwardly at the age of ten while outwardly to have grown the muscles of a healthy man of twenty-one. I came near to achieving the latter, at nineteen. But I had begun to "take books too seriously" and was reputed to be writing more than letters, and, what was worse, keeping it all to myself.

I could not dance and would not accompany my cousin to the larger yet uglier weekend dances, so different from the earlier ones haunted by joy and half-dynastic couplings. These later affairs were cruelly dismissive of the plain, or merely awkward; arenas of less than golden lads and girls who came to raise dust and a beer-glazed competitiveness, a perfumed and hair-oiled aquiescence among the young, no longer boys and girls—among largely unfriendly "couples" who came to bargain hard among themselves for a specious popularity. Some there were who came simply to dance to the awful music, the loud distorted echoes of the popular orchestras of the day that played "strict tempo" dance music. One or two brief attendances on my part taught me my place: back among the snoozing dogs before the winter fire or the empty summer grate in the sitting room. Alone, the elders gone to bed, musing over a book or a page of half-composed verses, dreaming of a dance in a nineteenth century ball-room out of the "Symphonie Fantastique"; equally as cruel and competitive, just as dismissive of the plain and shy, yet once again haunted by joy and despair and the hordes of selectively passionate forebears.

Perhaps it was the far-too-similar-to-the-urban aspect that dismayed me but the fact remains I was no companion to my cousin and no second son to my aunt—or if one, an unwanted one—and I was totally unaware of the pressures of failing health and already failed farming that settled down like a dusty sheet over, to me, the idyllic acres. I still could climb hills, no longer with my ferret-loving cousin admittedly, but if my uncle set me to scythe or brush-hook through a paddock marred prettily with fern I'd do it and in the right amount of time.

So subterranean factions were established and the facade of family flawed by my awkward, stubborn presence. A fair girl two farms away had smiled at me in passing on her pony. And then had come to our farm to pick peas and beat me and my unbeatable cousin, out of habit rather than a show of friendly force. I lingered with her, once again unattainably and prettily mounted on her little horse, once again that much up in the air, over my eager head, and once again she smiled warmly and it seemed to me then and now to invite further meetings. But I was told she had a suitor and he was favoured by her family, and besides she was such a truly good-natured girl she would smile at a dog.

I never saw her again but dreamt of her daily, nightly for months to come as a loving friend, as one to walk the fields and hillsides with, as a gentle lover, even. I'd have kissed her warm and generous lips in the pale face under the closed hazel eyes and under the short cornsilk coloured yet coarser hair. And I'd imagine the reassuring squeeze of her hand slipping from mine. If only I had spoken a few more words and asked to meet and walk or ride with her here and there, or had braved familial inspection and possible duel of knuckles with her suitor. If only. Now she would be a grandmother, or dead, or both, or single still, or somebody else, as I am—somebody else remembering the air, the hills, the nearly always green background of springing grass, tree, crop, and the blue white grey of sky, cloud, mountain stone, and everywhere about us the singing silences of the landscape's vibrant distances, bird thronged and animal packed, country silences punctuated and penetrated by lowings, barks, mews, shouts, crowings, twitterings, clucks, whinnyings, and the chug or whine of a lone motor.

And so from all these sad clashes with invoiced familial criticisms and even sadder non-communings I walked away occasionally and sometimes climbed a convenient hill, sometimes simply strolled about the never fully known acres, for each season showed a dozen different faces of field and waterflow of creaturely renewal and the earth and sky pasturing trees with their slower lives of breathing leafage, so that there was never need of argumentative confrontation but something like an armed truce developed and was mutually employed over the passing months without much damage to the already tentative relationships, the already diminished returns of affection, no different really to those encountered elsewhere, everywhere.

The only thing that did not basically reject my odd belonging was the land and, eventually, that last extension of the land's grudging goodwill, my uncle. One night in the shadowy farmhouse, aunt absent, cousin elsewhere, he exhibited in a shifting of lanterns a flickering kindness, a calm acceptance of my callous early manhood, so that I took to playing neverending games of cards with him in which I gladly but defensively lost. Unendingly, night after night I played the game, losing to him and making him in the process absentmindedly happy. Two handed five hundred or some such equally forgettable game, exercise of the instant mind. The distancing from his kin became obvious to me, though never to them. He walked and ploughed and milked the remaining acres of barely fertile land and largely unco-operative beasts but always in the knowledge of son and wife nearby and daughter safely elsewhere. I was his true apprentice in more than farming: he had his seizures, I my writing and deepening phases of joy and despair. He helped me continue to live, and so, with food and drink and partial acceptance, did the others.

But from time to time I had to leave them all to themselves and go hill-climbing or walking about the river flat, investigating the nearby island of raised earth and clustering trees that covered the bones of long dead cattle and may one time have been a real island in a watery surround of swamp and reed but was then an isle of the dead in the tides of earth and living grass. I had come once to it to get to the other side of things and stay forever, but had moved on and came to see it as another sign, a watershed along the way. It could never accommodate me or my needs but served to remind me that even graveyards grow green trees, and small lives move about the living boles, as life and death are intermingled.

Fields and the River

There was a special dispensation for small boys and girls in company
or alone to aimlessly wander or purposefully walk through planted fields
and along cattle tracks between them, sometimes on a level with
lucerne or corn stalks, sometimes higher than the stubble or green beginnings
though lower than the hoary fence posts or even the higher stands of the
frightful,
always chill barbed wire betufted with fragments of cowhide, sometimes
bloodied.
We crawled gingerly through or under these petrific, mechanical
blackberry vines
whose only fruit was flesh-blebs of animal and human, with hate
and a horrible respect. Sometimes the track between the fenced field
and paddock was sunken so that our heads were lower than the ploughed
earth.
Then our speech or even breathing became louder, more obvious than before.
This usually occurred as we approached the river's bank or a pebbled
crossing. And trees grew thick clustered about the water's verge, small oaks
and the occasional willow, but mostly a darker foliaged, darktrunked species
of pine, and among them though somehow separate, for trees and flowers
have their societal
peculiarities, the smooth grey trunked or the gingery gums, their topmost
foliage lost to us who were nose-high only to the very lowest
spirit-scribblings on their embraceably smooth and sensually rounded trunks
and lower limbs. The country boys must often have imagined as I did
a friendly nude woman of gigantic yet never wholly distorted
proportions languorously beckoning or merely witnessing the baring
of our winter whitened or summer browned boy bodies and miniature
sex, leaping
like small pale ghosts between the dark pats of cow dung on the stubbled
grass
avoiding the diabolical bindy-eye that pierced and painfully clung
to the leatheriest sole, a three pronged thorn that hid in grass and reminded
me
in appearance of a tiny cattle skull. Then uninterruptedly running

down the track splitting the bank's lip, the coarse particles of sandstone
becoming
sand and slush of mud and dung that led on to the river's raised
bed cobbled with rounded many-coloured stones, large as skulls,
small as avocado pits. The smoothest of all stones that I
had ever seen or felt, sun-warmed and strangely capable of causing
a pleasing ache in the down-pressed arch of the foot, reminded me of
the pebbles
scattered and clustered in Arthur Rackham's illustrations to Grimm and
Andersen
for these too lay half-hid and submerged among the exposed roots of trees
on the eroded bank and I peopled such places with the angular-limbed
and pot-bellied, pointed-nosed and sharp-eared creatures of fay.
But for the most we had only eyes for large birds or small rabbits,
and the occasional silver-grey flash of fish beneath the river's sunlit brown
or lucent flow that softly and caressingly surrounded us
with forefeelings of a lover's deepest embrace. The fresh water
softly clinging rather than penetrating to my salt-water seasoned
self so that I imagined at times I was swimming in a huge, half-set
jelly. At other times the underlying cold came piercingly up
from clinging mud and swiftly entrapping streamers of weed that we had
been warned of
and that once I had felt entwine about my feet as sucking supple as
an octopus. I had just managed to kick free without the shame
of panicking outwardly before the shouting, splashing, floating, diving
others whose pallid cheerful faces laughed, crowed and grimaced at the small
moonlike rounded bums that sometimes surfaced in lieu of a well known head.
Then all would dreamily adjourn to a long bank of golden sand
and grey overlapping mud at the river's placid centre, a raised place
to lie on and take the sun's heat, tempered by river cool and leaf filtered shade
until the gradual overturning of bodily comfort drove us drowsily
to re-enter the Nirvana of the cooling river. But afterwards,
unlike the effect of the salt ocean's astringencies, we felt a dozing
mood upon us and the clothes strangely rough and oppressive after
the embraces of the air and water. The girls who sometimes accompanied us
did not laugh at us or we at them, but rather over athletic feats
attempted and as often failed. Sometimes a girl would fierily challenge,
defeating us or failing beside us in mutual wallowings of laughter

or mock-anger. They would all be thickened or thinned by middle-age now.
But then they were pink and angular or chubby bodies with shouting mouths
or concentratedly silent heads. And to lie beside them on the baking
sandbank, watching the pale green leaves of the small willow that had
taken root there
unmoving in the sparkling air, or to swim and float and tussle with them,
the oblique thrill of touch not troubling us but surreptitiously sought
among each other, this was to live fully in the goodwill of the moment.
Afterwards some would scramble, three or four at a time, onto the long
broad back of a patiently waiting draught-horse and move off slowly
up one of the bank's intertwining tracks, while others would retrace the paths
between the sleeping-waking fields and cow-thronged paddocks to this or that
homestead and a mug of tea and the inescapable afternoon milking.
These field traversing and river swimming episodes were always no more
than partial holidays for those children, and every farm was keyed to the
constant
labour of the elders and partial yet continuing labour of
the young. We were so childish as to hardly comprehend the necessities
of such behaviour, the reiterated employments, but barely accepted as
habitual encroachments on our first and always seeming world of sensation
and waking dream. If we paused on returning from the generous ever-
flowing river
to the cow-yard or the house to track a rabbit or look for fresh burrows
or merely traces of the black pellets that betrayed their nearby and constant
presence
I would be visually transfixed in full search by the uprearing chassis
of a rusting machine. To leave these surrogate animals where they stopped
was apparently
sensible, but not to cover them with a tarpaulin or hessian bags
seemed callous in the extreme. The rust-brown metal seat, the bulky belly
of the exposed engine, the circular concavities of multiple blades,
all beaded with rust, the great complex hand grab of metal claws—
I would return with my accepting cousin and fretfully remember
beyond the no-time of swimming the river and strolling underneath its trees
the days and months of the labouring fields, the stark patience of the
machines.

The Hunting Girl

Once at bright mid-morning on an easy weekend day
coming down from the hill paddock I saw the girl Laura,
daughter of the neighbouring farmer's assistant, a brown skinned girl
with yellow hair, limbs long and stick-thin as a young Aboriginal's,
overlarge bare feet planted firmly at the creek's edge,
all of her poised and balanced to propel a home-made spear
longer than herself and tipped with a wire-fastened knife-blade
into the seemingly empty and shallow waterflow, I assumed
she was playing at her brothers' games and stopped chasing heifers
down the hill, making them dance about, and watched as she poised,
flexed and threw the spear into the quietly moving water.
Then, tucking her cotton dress into her plain white underwear,
she waded in after the upright spear. She did not seem so thin
then, her thighs exposed seemed fuller, rounder, and her legs
slim rather than thin. I sat on the grass a little way off
and concentratedly watched her natural balletic movements.
Back on the bank Laura re-arranged her dress and I thought
she must have seen me but, no, after another lunging throw
into the centre of the creek she tucked her dress in again,
high up on her thighs, the white underwear clung and now I noticed
the widening hips and shapely small buttocks. But Laura and I
had trodden down the silage in friendly silence many a time.
I knew the way her yellow hair tufted at the back
and how she would suddenly brush the front strands from her freckled
forehead,
and the pale blue eyes would lower with the very slightest rising
of the wide mouth's corners. Her nose was not small yet attractively upturned
and stamped with freckles. She was not the kind of girl I'd begun to dream of
at about her age, but neither was any other that I'd seen.
I wondered then what kind of boy she dreamed of, or if any,
as she poised and lunged and waded to retrieve the unwieldy spear.
She seemed intent on hunting and to have no other thought
or feeling save to aim and throw as best she could, and to spear
an eel. Then the spear fell sideways in the water and she leapt,

untucked dress and all, in after the waving wood, for the blade
had transfixed something that moved. I nearly ran to help, but knew
she needed none, she was the mistress of the situation.
She emerged with a medium sized eel wriggling at the end of the spear.
Driving it into earth to pinion it, she placed one large bare foot
behind the eel's head, and drew a hunting knife from the grassy bank
and hacked the live eel's head off. Then she stood aside to wring out
her dampened dress and briefly smile—or it seemed a smile—towards me.
I summoned up a gesture, half salute, half wave. She appeared
to nod, then took her spear, her knife, her catch, both severed head
and the still slightly writhing body, back along the creek's
edge towards the other farm. She never looked back once.
I came down to her hunting—I cannot call it fishing—place
and saw the blood upon the wettened grass and stood there musing
how I so full of Endymion should come upon a true
Diana and not say a word but merely witness her prowess,
and the beauty of her brown and rounding thighs, the summer moonlight
of her hair, the pallid summer dawning of her woken eyes.
Would she have rounded breasts beneath her dress? I had thought her
earlier
a living marionette, a girl Pinocchio; had liked her
but not engaged her interest. I realised then the man
she would consider was so unlike me that I had been to her
but one of the other farm boys, an elder brother, a part companion,
touchable even in the silo's privacy. How I longed
for such another opportunity, but the silage was packed
and cooking itself. I watched for her then and saw her often enough,
even spoke a kind of half-speech, words about the farm and its peoples,
never about ourselves. I did not dream about Laura but she
had become a kind of muse to me. Poised between girl and woman,
she bled at times and was unafraid, and silent. Now her silences,
the faint smile and the unreadable pale blue eyes, the thin
yet rounding body, stayed with me—not obsessing, but making me
want the company of such women, calm yet inwardly passionate,
capable of the sudden precipitate plunge, the unstudied action.
Though I feared to think of the eel's beheading, my own sex shrivelling at
the thought of such an obvious symbol. No, not then so consciously
apprehended, more a shocked distaste at the callous necessity.

I was appalled at the killing yet it was natural and swift.
I realise I might have dreamt of meeting her naked, of rising to
the brown thighs' darker centre, of receiving a kiss that pinned
and then emasculated me—but I didn't, then or afterwards.
The truth of what I had seen remained sufficient in itself.
Laura must have come again to the creek at the foot of the slope,
but I never witnessed her more than once, so perfectly attuned
to who she was and what she was doing; a truly intuitive huntress
food gathering for herself and her father's hungry family.
In a short while I had left the farm forever and never forgot.